The ultimate kings of seduction!

THE PLAYBOYS AND HEROES COLLECTION

The Playboys and Heroes large print collection
gives you lavish stories of luxury
from your favourite top authors
in easier-to-read print.

ROYAL AFFAIRS: CARETTI'S FORCED BRIDE

Jennie Lucas

First published in Great Britain 2008
by Mills & Boon, an imprint of Harlequin (UK) Limited,
Large Print edition 2012
Harlequin (UK) Limited,
Eton House, 18-24 Paradise Road, Richmond, Surrey TW9 1SR

© Jennie Lucas 2008

ISBN: 978 0 263 23052 9

Harlequin (UK) policy is to use papers that are natural, renewable
and recyclable products and made from wood grown in sustainable
forests. The logging and manufacturing process conform to the
legal environmental regulations of the country of origin.

Printed and bound in Great Britain
by CPI Antony Rowe, Chippenham, Wiltshire

Jennie Lucas grew up dreaming about faraway lands. At fifteen, hungry for experience beyond the borders of her small Idaho city, she went to a Connecticut boarding school on scholarship. She took her first solo trip to Europe at sixteen, then put off college and travelled around the USA, supporting herself with jobs as diverse as petrol station cashier and newspaper advertising assistant.

At twenty-two, she met the man who would be her husband. After their marriage, she graduated from Kent State with a degree in English. Seven years after she started writing, she got the magical call from London that turned her into a published author.

Since then life has been hectic, with a new writing career, a sexy husband and two babies under two, but she's having a wonderful (albeit sleepless) time. She loves immersing herself in dramatic, glamorous, passionate stories. Maybe she can't physically travel to Morocco or Spain right now, but for a few hours a day, while her children are sleeping, she can be there in her books.

Jennie loves to hear from her readers. You can visit her website at www.jennielucas.com, or drop her a note at jennie@jennielucas.com

CHAPTER ONE

CLIMBING out of his Rolls-Royce, Paolo Caretti pulled his black coat close to his body and stepped out onto the sidewalk. Sunrise was just a slash of scarlet above New York's gray skyline as his chauffeur held an umbrella to block the freezing rain.

"Paolo. Wait."

For a moment he thought he'd imagined the soft sound, that his insomnia had finally caused him to dream in daytime. Then a small figure stepped out from behind the tall metal sculpture that decorated the front of his twenty-story office building. Rain plastered the woman's hair and clothes to her body. Her face was pale with cold. She must have been standing outside of his building for hours, waiting for him.

"Don't turn me away," she said. "Please."

Her voice was soft, throaty, low. Just like he remembered. After all these years he still remembered everything about her, no matter how much money he made or how many mistresses he'd taken to wipe her from his memory.

His jaw tightened. "You shouldn't have come."

"I…I need your help." Princess Isabelle de Luceran took a deep breath, her light brown eyes shimmering beneath the streetlights. "Please. I have nowhere else to go."

Their gazes locked. For a moment he was taken back to spring days picnicking in Central Park, to summer nights making love in his Little Italy apartment. When, for four sweet months, she'd made his world bright and new and he'd asked her to be his wife…

Now, he looked at her coldly. "Make an appointment."

He started to step around her, but she blocked him. "I've tried. I've left ten messages with your secretary. Didn't she give them to you?"

Valentina had, but he'd ignored them. Isabelle de Luceran meant nothing to him. He'd stopped wanting her long ago.

Or so he'd told himself. But now her beauty was seeping through him like a poison. Her expressive hazel eyes, her full mouth, those lush curves hidden beneath the ladylike coat—he remembered everything. The taste of her skin. The feel of her lips kissing down his belly. Her soft hands stroking between his legs…

"You're alone?" He clenched his jaw, struggling to get himself under control. "Where are your bodyguards?"

"I left them at the hotel," she whispered. "Help me. Please. For the sake of…who we once were."

To his horror, he saw tears blending with rain to fall in rivulets down her cheek. Isabelle?

Crying? Her hands trembled. Whatever she wanted, she must want it badly, he thought.

Good. Having her on her knees begging for a favor was a very pleasant image. It wouldn't make up for what she'd done, but it might be a start.

Abruptly, he moved closer, tracing a finger down her wet cheek. "You want a favor?" Her skin felt cold, as if she were indeed the ice princess the world believed her to be. "You know I'll make you pay for it."

"Yes." Her voice was so quiet he could barely hear her over the sound of rain. "I know."

"Follow me." Taking the umbrella from his chauffeur, he turned on his heel and strode up the wide concrete steps. As he entered through his building's revolving door, he nodded a greeting to the security guards in the foyer. He could hear the click-click-click of Isabelle's high-heeled boots across the marble floor behind him.

"Good morning, Salvatore," Paolo said to the first security guard.

"Good morning." The elderly man cleared his throat. "It's a cold one today, isn't it, Signor Caretti? Makes me wish I was in the old country, where it's warmer." His eyes trailed to Isabelle. "Or San Piedro, maybe."

So even Salvatore had recognized her. Paolo uneasily wondered what his executive secretary would do. Valentina Novak, though highly competent, had one weakness: celebrity tabloids. And Isabelle, the princess of a tiny Mediterranean kingdom, was one of the most famous women in the world.

As Paolo left the guard station, he heard Salvatore whistle through his teeth. He couldn't blame the man. Isabelle had been a lovely, fresh-faced girl at eighteen; she was more beautiful now. As if even time itself were in love with her.

Angrily shaking the thought away, Paolo strode to his private elevator and pressed the button for the penthouse level. As soon as the elevator's doors closed, he turned to her.

"All right. Let's have it."

Isabelle's voice was low. Desperate. "Alexander's been kidnapped."

"Your nephew?" He gave her an incredulous stare. "Kidnapped?"

"You're the only one who can save him!"

His eyebrows rose, still disbelieving. "The heir to the throne of San Piedro? Needs *my* help?"

"He's not just the heir now. He's the King." She shook her head, wiping her eyes. "My brother and sister-in-law died two weeks ago. You must have heard."

"Yes." He'd unwillingly heard the details from Valentina, who'd told him the couple had died in a boating accident in Majorca, leaving their nine-year-old son behind. And that wasn't the only gossip she'd shared…

Grinding his teeth, he pushed the troubling thought away. "I'm sorry."

"My mother is officially regent until he comes of age, but she's getting older, and I'm trying to help." She took a deep breath. "I was at the London economic summit yesterday when I got a frantic call from Alexander's nanny. Alexander was missing. Then I received a letter demanding I meet the kidnapper at midnight tonight. Alone."

"Don't tell me you're actually considering following his instructions?"

"If you don't help me, I don't know what else to do."

"Your nephew has a national army, bodyguards, police. Get them involved at once."

She shook her head. "The letter said if I contact anyone in an official capacity I'll never see Alexander again!"

He gave a harsh laugh. "Of course the kidnapper would say that. Don't be a fool. You don't need my help. Go to your police. Let them handle it." As the *ding* sounded and the doors opened on the penthouse level, he turned away from her. "Go home, Isabelle."

"Wait." She put her hand on his wrist. "There's more. Something I haven't told you."

He stared down at her hand. He could feel the electricity through his cashmere coat, his tailored jacket, his finely cut shirt. He had the sudden desire to close the door behind him, to push her up against the wall of the elevator, to pull up her skirt and taste her. He yearned to lick the rain off her skin, to pull off her sodden clothes and warm her with the length of his body…

What the hell was wrong with him? He felt nothing for Isabelle de Luceran but scorn— both for her shallow nature and for the naïve boy he'd been when he'd loved her.

So how was it possible that five minutes with her made his body combust into flame? Even through his clothes, her touch burned his skin.

He jerked his arm away.

"I'll give you one minute," he ground out. "Don't waste it."

He strode out onto his private floor, crowded with employees who managed his global holdings. Valentina stood up from her desk. As always, she was the picture of well-groomed efficiency: her stylish red suit accentuated her curvy figure, and her bright auburn hair was pulled back in a neat chignon. Her only jewelry was the gold Tiffany watch he'd given her last Christmas.

"Good morning, Mr. Caretti." She spoke rapidly, chewing on her full lower lip with white, even teeth. "Here are the numbers you wanted from the Rome office. Palladium is up two percent on the Nymex, and I've taken several calls this morning from reporters about the rumor of a buyout offer. Then, of course, all those calls from a woman claiming to be…"

Blue eyes widening, she sucked in her breath, staring at Isabelle.

"You told them Caretti Motors is not for sale," Paolo said. "Correct?"

The thirty-year-old redhead looked as if she might swoon. "Yes. No. That is—"

"Hold my calls," he bit out. Grabbing Isabelle's wrist, he dragged her into his office and closed the door behind them. Tossing his coat on the plush black leather sofa, he turned on a small lamp to illuminate the dark, spacious room.

"Thank you," Isabelle said softly, rubbing her wrist. "I appreciate that you—"

"Say what you have to say, and get out," he interrupted.

Her caramel-colored eyes narrowed. She took a deep breath. "I need your help."

"So you said," he replied coldly. "But you didn't explain why you need *my* help instead of going to the police or the bodyguards who protect San Piedro's king. Or, better yet," he added scornfully, "your fiancé."

She looked at him in surprise. "You know about Magnus?"

Paolo folded his arms, trying to calm the tension he felt in every muscle. "You're famous, Isabelle. I hear about your life whether I want to or not."

But it was more than that.

Isabelle.

And Magnus.

Together.

He was still reeling. Ever since Valentina had started sighing over their "glamorous" affair, he'd wanted to hit something—preferably Magnus's meek, handsome face.

"I'm sorry," she said in a small voice. "I don't try to end up in the tabloids. They chase me. It's how they sell papers."

His lip curled.

"It must be hard," he agreed sardonically. He could hardly believe she was trying to pretend she didn't love every minute of her fame. Her whole shallow existence had been built on the temple of her vanity and insatiable appetite for adoration. Even he himself had once been stupid enough to—

Stopping the thought cold, he clenched his jaw. "So why don't you ask your fiancé for help?"

"He's not my fiancé. Not yet."

"But he soon will be."

For the first time she looked away. "He proposed to me a few days ago. I haven't given him my answer yet, but I will. Once Alexander is safe, we will announce our engagement."

It was exactly what he'd expected, and yet involuntarily, he stepped toward her. Isabelle—Magnus's bride? The thought ricocheted through his body like a bullet.

"And as for why I can't ask him for help," she said, "he would insist on calling in the police and working through proper channels." She shook her head fiercely. "I can't be that patient. Not when some criminal has Alexander."

The irony of it rose like bile in his throat, nearly choking him. "So that's why you've come to me?"

"I've read about you as well." Her eyes met his. "You're ruthless. Well-connected. Magnus has told me about—"

"About what?" he interrupted harshly.

"About how you focus only on yourself," she said. "You ignore the pain of others. You'll drive right past accidents. You're almost inhuman in your determination to win."

He clenched his jaw. Of course Magnus hadn't told her about their past—he was even more ashamed of it than Paolo was. "That's why I always win every race and Magnus takes second place."

"People whisper that…you're truly your father's son," she said quietly.

He'd heard it so many times that he didn't even flinch. "So you're seeking one monster without morals to fight another?"

"Yes."

"Thank you."

"Alexander's bodyguards could be involved. I need an outsider, and you're the only one ruthless enough to bring him home safe. No one must ever know he was kidnapped. It would make my country appear weak and corrupt—as if we couldn't even protect our king."

"So you want me to keep the whole thing secret, even from your future husband?" He raised an eyebrow. "Hardly a sound foundation for marriage, Princess."

"Insult me however you want. Just bring Alexander home!"

He watched her. "And you're sure Magnus didn't send you to ask me?"

"Of course not." She lifted her chin. "He would be horrified if he knew. He wouldn't want me to get involved."

"Such a perfect gentleman," he said sardonically.

She bristled. "He *is* perfect! He's handsome and charming. Wealthy and influential beyond belief. The tenth richest man in the world!"

"I always knew you'd sell yourself to the highest bidder, Isabelle."

"Just as I always knew you'd replace me with the cheapest-looking tart you could find," she snapped. "I'm just surprised it took you a whole hour."

He exhaled with a flare of nostril. The night Isabelle had so abruptly ended their affair he'd gotten drunk and slept with his next-door neighbor—a girl trying to break into Broadway whose name he could no longer remember. For a moment he wondered how Isabelle knew about it. Then he decided he didn't care.

"What did you expect me to do?" he replied acidly. "Spend my whole life celibate? Mourning your loss?"

A pink flush stained her cheeks. "No," she muttered. "That would be pathetic." She bit her bottom lip, and in spite of his dislike he couldn't help but be aroused. Her lips looked tender. Full. And he remembered their sweetness. It had been so many years, and yet he could still remember how those lips had felt, kissing down the length of his body…

"Of course a man like you couldn't be faithful for longer than a day." She straightened her shoulders, haughtily raising her chin. "It's why I'm glad I found a man I can trust."

As she'd obviously never trusted *him*. Paolo's hands clenched. He had to change the subject before he lost control and did something utterly insane…like grab Isabelle by the shoulders and kiss her until she forgot Magnus and every other man she'd taken to her bed in the last ten years. Before he made love to her right here on his desk, punishing her, pleasuring her, branding her forever as his own.

"Go ask Prince Charming for help, then," he said harshly.

"He can't help me. I told you. You're the only one who can." She took a deep breath. "Please, Paolo. I know that I hurt you…"

"You didn't hurt me." He glanced out the wide windows. From the view on the twentieth floor, misty clouds hung low over the city, covering it like a shroud. "Just tell me one thing—who benefits from your nephew's kidnapping?"

Her eyelashes fluttered against her cheek. "Politically? No one. We're a small country."

"Ransom?"

"That has to be it. But if the kidnapper asks for a large sum, it will be hard for us to pay it. We cannot raise taxes when half our factories have moved offshore. Our economy is struggling. If it weren't for tourism…"

"Struggling?" He looked at her pearls, her designer coat, her expensive high-heeled boots.

She flushed. "My clothes are given to me free by designers. Everyone wants publicity." She glanced uneasily at the door. "Speaking of which—would any of your employees call the press about my visit?"

"I trust them implicitly." And, unfortunately, he also trusted that as soon as Valentina had recovered her senses she'd started phoning all her friends in the Tri-State area. She was normally the epitome of discretion, but with her passion for celebrities there was just no way she'd be able to keep silent. "Let's make this quick. What about Magnus?"

"Magnus?"

"Would he have any reason to kidnap your nephew?"

Her eyes widened in shock. "No! Why would he?"

"Perhaps he wants his own children to inherit the throne."

She looked at him like he was mad. "His children?"

"His future children. With you."

Their eyes met.

"Oh," she whispered. "Those children."

An echo of primal, almost animal fury went through him at the thought of Isabelle pregnant with another man's child. Once he would have killed any man who'd tried to touch her...

She exhaled. "I love San Piedro. You know I do. We're rich in culture and tradition. But we're just three square miles. Magnus owns more land in Austria alone. The von Trondhem bloodline dates back to Charlemagne."

"Are you trying to convince me to marry him, or yourself?" he said acidly.

She looked at him. "He's a good man."

"Right." Forced to concede her point, he scowled. He'd raced against Magnus von Trondhem for five years now on the circuit of the Motorcycle Grand Prix. And as far as he could tell he really was a Boy Scout—the kind who was afraid to tilt his motorcycle an extra degree in a turn beyond what the manual advised. The son of an Austrian prince, rich and respected, he was also bland and boring enough to let Isabelle lead him by the nose.

The perfect husband for Isabelle, he thought. The husband she deserved. And yet...

"So will you help me?" she whispered.

Help her? Paolo didn't want to go near her. Just looking at her from a few paces away made his whole body rise. Her skin looked soft, so soft. Her beige wool coat, belted at the waist, accentuated her petite, curvaceous figure. He could see the rapid pulse of her slender throat beneath her old-fashioned pearls. And she still used the same lotion, the same shampoo: he caught the delicate scent of Provençal roses and Mediterranean oranges. The scent, which he remembered so well, made him instantly hard.

And he realized two things.

First: he hadn't forgotten her. Not by a long shot. He yearned for her like a starving man longed for bread.

Second: there was no way in hell he was going to let another man have her.

He wanted to take her to bed until he'd had his fill. Until his desire for her was completely satiated.

Until he could toss her aside as carelessly as she'd once discarded him.

"Please," she whispered. Her tawny skin was pale with cold and her long chestnut hair was wet with rain, but when she looked up her eyes were the color of honey in paradise. She placed her small hand over his larger one. "Will you?"

For a moment he looked down at her hand. Then, with a shudder of desire, he looked out the windows, towards the Hudson River and all of Manhattan beneath him. The sun had risen at last, trickling pale and wan through the gloom. Far below, he could see taxis crawling down the street, and pedestrians scurrying ant-like down sidewalks. Dreary and dark, the city was endless shades of gray.

Except for her. Even desperate, wet and cold, she glowed with color and light. Even in the belted coat, she drew him with her heat. Made him yearn and feel.

Made him realize that every woman he'd been with for the last ten years had been a pale imitation.

He tried to remember the last time he'd felt this way. But all he could recall was making love to her long ago in his dingy one-room apartment in Little Italy, far from her dorm at Barnard College. He remembered the way she'd felt when he touched her. The way she'd tasted. Her sweetness, the beads of sweat on her skin. His mattress on the floor—the sound of the springs moving beneath her body. The slow, quiet whir of the fan. And the heat. Most of all the heat.

Paolo's eyes suddenly narrowed.

Ten years was long enough.

He still desired her.

So he would have her.

"Paolo?"

"Very well." He turned back to her carelessly. "I'll help you. I'll save your nephew. I'll keep it quiet. And I will destroy any man who tries to stop me."

Her eyes flashed relief. "Thank you, Paolo. I knew you would—"

"And in return—" he looked down at her with dark eyes "—you will be my mistress."

His mistress?

Isabelle stared at him in horror. "You can't be serious."

He gave her a brief, humorless smile. "You have some objection to becoming my lover? Strange. You had no objections before. In fact, you did it for pleasure, with no return favor required."

It was heartless of him to remind her of that. Lover? The word was meaningless on his sensual, lying lips. Paolo Caretti didn't know anything about love. And she certainly couldn't trust him. He'd proved that long ago. So why was she surprised to discover he still had no heart?

"One thing hasn't changed," she choked out. "You're still as selfish as ever."

"More so." He came closer to her, his eyes as dark and fathomless as the midnight sea. "You would enjoy being in my bed. I promise you."

She shivered as he reached out to stroke a long tendril of her hair. He might know nothing of love, but pleasure was another matter. Darkly handsome, he had the same strong physique, the same broad shoulders she remembered. The same Roman profile and chiseled jawline. The same dark, intense eyes.

It was true he now wore a black Savile Row suit instead of a blue mechanic's jumpsuit, and his fingernails were clean instead of dirty with engine grease, but he was more dangerous to her than ever.

Because Paolo wasn't just her first. He was

her only. And if she spent time with him she would risk far more than her heart…

"No," she whispered. "I can't. I'll give you anything else you want, but not that."

He turned back toward his desk, dismissing her. "Good luck finding your nephew."

She swallowed. She was at his mercy and she knew it. She would pay any price to cuddle Alexander close again. To have him squirm in her embrace like always, his sweet, exasperated voice complaining, "Aunt Isabelle, I'm not a little boy anymore!"

But, king or not, he *was* a little boy. He always would be to her—though he'd grown up far too quickly over the last two weeks. Every morning he'd met Isabelle and his grandmother at the breakfast table red-eyed with grief, but she hadn't seen him cry. He'd gone through the motions of his new royal duties with quiet dignity, showing the type of man he would someday become. The king San Piedro needed.

So it was pointless to pretend there was anything she wouldn't do to save him. Even sell herself to Paolo Caretti, the one man she'd sworn to avoid for the rest of her life.

But…she couldn't become Paolo's mistress. In addition to her own private reasons for wanting to stay away from Paolo, nothing must prevent her marriage to Prince Magnus von Trondhem. Since the textiles industry had moved offshore, San Piedro had been in economic freefall. They desperately needed the influx of business and money that Magnus would provide. Without it, more factories would close. More shops would go bankrupt. More families would be desperate.

Isabelle rubbed her eyes. She couldn't let that happen. She had to save Alexander. Save her country. Compared to that, her own feelings—her own *life*—meant nothing.

"I can't be your mistress," she said quietly. "I am engaged to be married."

"No, you're not. Not yet. You said so yourself."

She shook her head. "That's just a technicality."

"Suit yourself," he said, turning away from her. "If you'll excuse me…"

"Wait."

He looked at her, raising a dark eyebrow.

She swallowed. He had her, and they both knew it. "One night," she said, nearly choking on the words. "I'll give you one night."

"One night?" He lifted her chin. "And you would give yourself to me completely?"

"Yes," she whispered, unable to meet his eyes.

She waited for waves of guilt to crush her at the thought of cheating on her future fiancé. Even though she was being blackmailed, even though it was to save a child, shouldn't she feel horrible at the thought of deceiving the perfect man she was to marry? After all, she above all people had seen the damage that infidelity could do.

But her heart felt nothing.

Because I don't love Magnus, she thought.

And I know he doesn't love me. The one small blessing in all of this.

To save Alexander, Isabelle would give herself to Paolo for one night. That was nothing. To save her country, she would soon give herself to Magnus for the rest of her life.

And she would forever keep secrets from them both…

"One night?" Paolo mused. "You hold yourself very high."

A very unladylike curse went through Isabelle's mind. "A child is in danger. If you were any sort of gentleman you wouldn't ask me to be your mistress as the price for your help!"

"He's not my child," he said coolly. "He's King of San Piedro, with a hundred bodyguards at his beck and call. You could have half of Europe searching for him already, but you chose to come to me instead." He came closer. "And, as you have already pointed out to me so succinctly, I'm not a gentleman."

His gaze devoured her whole. He leaned forward, his lips inches from hers. She could feel the muscles of his thighs pressing against her legs. Her knees felt weak. She hadn't eaten or slept for two days. She'd barely made it to New York without the paparazzi catching her, and ditching her bodyguards at the hotel hadn't been easy. All she'd been able to think about was Alexander. Where was he? Was he being well treated? Was he scared and alone?

Paolo was right. She didn't need a gentleman. She didn't need someone who was kind and civilized and knew how to properly tie a cravat.

She needed a hard-edged warrior who was strong and ruthless. She needed a man who was invincible.

She needed Paolo.

But at what cost? How much was she willing to risk?

"Why do you want me in your bed?" she

whispered. "To soothe your pride? To punish me? You could have any woman you wanted!"

"I know." He ran his hand down the side of her neck to the bare skin of her collarbone above her wool coat. "I want you."

Hearing him speak those words made her weak, and his fingertips caused heat to sweep across her body like a brush fire. How many nights had she dreamed of him—reliving every moment he'd ever taken her in his arms? How many days, while sitting through long speeches that would make any sane person want to stab herself with a pencil, had she fantasized about the way he'd once touched her?

For ten years she'd longed for him. Even knowing he was forbidden to her forever. Even knowing that if she gave herself to him again it would risk far more than her marriage. Far more than her heart.

"Why?" she managed. "Why me?"

He shrugged. "Perhaps I want to possess something other men only dream of."

"Possess?" At that, she raised her chin. "Even if I become your mistress, you will never truly possess me, Paolo. Never."

He looked down at her, his eyes dark. "Ah. Now there's the Princess I remember. I knew you couldn't stay a meek little mouse for long." He stroked her cheek. "But we both know you're lying. You *will* give yourself to me. And not just for your nephew's sake, but because you want to. Because you cannot resist."

She couldn't deny it. Not when just his slightest touch sent her senses reeling, made her body combust beneath the chill of her wet clothes.

"Would you keep our night a secret?" she asked in a low voice. "Could you?"

His lip curled. "You mean, would I call reporters to brag about my good fortune?"

"That's not what—" She took a deep breath.

"No one must know that Alexander was ever kidnapped. And my marriage…"

"I get it." Clenching his jaw, he held out his hand. "Let me see the letter."

She gave him the scribbled note out of her coat pocket. Isabelle already knew it by heart, the strangely formed letters demanding that she go alone to the palace garden in San Piedro at midnight tonight and tell no one.

"How did you get this?"

"It was left outside the door of my suite at the Savoy."

"You haven't left yourself much time," he said, handing the letter back to her. "What was your plan if I refused?"

"I don't know."

"No other plans? No one else to ask for help?" he said softly. "Perhaps I should demand more of you. A month of nights. A year of them."

Horrified, she stared up at him.

He gave her a smile. "Fortunately for you, I

tire of women easily. One night with you should be more than enough." He stroked her cheek, the edge of her jawline, the sensitive crook of her neck. "And so you agree to the terms?"

She pressed her hands against her belly. She wanted to say yes. And, if she were truly honest with herself, it wasn't just to save Alexander.

But it was too dangerous. Giving herself to Paolo, even for one night, risked everything she held dear—her marriage to Magnus, her heart and, worst of all, her secret. Dear God, her secret…

"Please, Paolo." She licked her dry lips. "Isn't there any other way you'd consider—"

He cut her off with a kiss. His lips crushed hers as his tongue penetrated her mouth, mastering her, enslaving her.

"Say yes," he growled. He kissed her again. "Say yes, damn you."

"Yes," she whispered, sagging in his arms.

He abruptly let her go. She nearly lost her

balance as he opened his cell phone and dialed. "Bertolli. Get every man on the list. Yes, I said every man. I will pay ten times the going rate. It must be flawless. Tonight."

Knees shaking, she sank into a chair, feeling as if she'd sold her very soul. She watched as he efficiently and effortlessly organized the invasion of her country. He turned away, barking orders into the phone, all business. As if he'd already forgotten she was there.

But she knew he hadn't forgotten her. He could feel her, as she could feel him.

She touched her lips. She'd spent ten years trying to forget Paolo Caretti. She'd given up what she loved most in order to stay out of his ruthless, vicious world. But now she was being drawn back in. She could only pray she wouldn't be irrevocably caught in his web.

His mistress for one night. That was the price. She would be used at his will and at his pleasure. And, worse still, he would make sure she enjoyed it. Just thinking of what was ahead, she clutched the arms of her chair as the world seemed to hover and spin around her.

All she could do now was pray that Paolo never discovered the secret she'd been hiding. The greatest secret of her life.

CHAPTER TWO

THE moon was hazy and full over the palace garden as Isabelle sat on a bench inside the hedge maze.

She shivered. She was still wearing the same blouse and skirt, covered by the belted wool coat, that she'd worn since she'd abruptly left London for New York. She was exhausted, grimy, and most of all she was afraid.

Afraid that at any moment Alexander's kidnapper would come out of the dark shadows like a wraith.

Afraid he wouldn't, and she'd lose him forever.

Paolo will find him, she told herself fiercely. Paolo Caretti was vicious and ruthless. If half the rumors were true, he was nothing like the young mechanic who'd once spoken of his father's criminal ties with revulsion, who'd seemed determined to build an honest life for himself.

Her mother had been right. *Blood will tell.*

But then, Isabelle had known Paolo couldn't be trusted from the moment when, mere hours after he'd proposed to her, he'd jumped into bed with another woman…

A twig snapped behind a far hedge. She leapt to her feet, her high-heeled boots sinking into the soft grass.

Don't be afraid, she repeated to herself, trying to steady the beat of her heart, the clammy shake of her hands. Don't be afraid.

"Who's there?" she whispered, despising the tremble in her voice.

No answer. Paolo had gone into Provence chasing a lead, but twenty of his men, along with her two most trusted bodyguards, were hidden invisibly throughout the garden. They awaited the kidnapper like death on gossamer wings.

In spite of that, she stared at the shadowy hedge with all her might, hardly able to breathe. All she could see was moonlight on dark green leaves. She could smell eucalyptus and pine, and hear the roar of the sea pounding the nearby cliffs.

Suddenly she heard voices in the darkness, a crash, rapidly running footsteps.

It's Paolo, she thought, her heart in her throat. He's come to tell me that Alexander's dead.

She closed her eyes, remembering the feel of the little boy's arms around her. Remembering his sweet face when she'd rocked him to sleep as a baby. The sound of his laugh as he'd toddled down the marble hallways of the *palais* on unsteady feet. If Alexander was dead, she didn't want to live. She squeezed her eyes shut, swaying on her feet. *Please let him be all right. Please. I'll do anything. Just let him be all right…*

"Aunt Isabelle!"

Her eyes flew open as she felt the little boy's arms around her.

"Alexander," she whispered. Pulling back, she looked at him in the moonlight, felt his cold, thin arms, saw the big grin on the face that was usually serious and pale. "Alexander," she breathed, and at that moment she realized she was weeping. "You're here. You're safe."

The boy gestured to Paolo, who was standing behind him like a dark guardian angel. "He found me. I'm fine, Aunt Isabelle! *Zut alors.*" He grimaced, squirming in her arms. "You're squashing me! I'm not a little baby, you know!"

"No, you're not," she agreed, smiling until her cheeks hurt. Tears were streaming down her face.

Behind him, Paolo folded his arms. "We tracked him to an abandoned *mas* thirty miles from here. He was tied to a chair in the farmhouse's unheated cellar. But he never cried—

not once." He glanced down at Alexander. "You're a brave kid."

Man and boy faced each other. They had similar coloring. The same dark eyes and dark hair. The same penetrating frown as they each took the other's measure.

Alexander shook his head. "There's no point in being afraid." His voice wobbled a little as he added, "When you're King, you do what you have to do."

He was repeating a phrase that Isabelle had heard her brother say many times. Though a faithless husband, he'd been a wonderful father. Maxim had loved Alexander so much. But then, he and Karin had spent so many years trying to have a child.

"Thank you for saving me, *monsieur*," the boy said, sounding far too old for his age—like a medieval king speaking to one of his knights.

"It was nothing," Paolo replied gruffly, taking off his black cashmere coat and slinging it over the boy's shivering shoulders. He turned to the man beside him. "Bertolli, take the King back to the palace as quietly as possible. Go through a side door and ask for…?" He looked at Isabelle.

"Milly Lavoisier," she said. "His nanny."

Alexander's face lit up. "Yes. Milly. She'll be missing me." He gave them a mischievous grin, and for the first time looked like a nine-year-old child. "She'll give me ice cream for this. For sure."

"Alexander, Milly knows the truth," Isabelle said, "but you must keep this a secret from everyone else. People must think you went on a skiing trip with me."

"I know, Aunt Isabelle." The boy drew himself up with dignity. "I can keep a secret."

"Of course you can." The boy was a de Luceran, after all. Secrets were the family trademark.

But there was a catch in her throat as she kissed his forehead. She held him tight in a hug, but was forced to let him go when he pulled away impatiently. The boy disappeared through the hedge maze with Bertolli, musing aloud over the flavors of ice cream he would choose, and whether Milly would give him two scoops or if he should try for three.

"You were right," Paolo said after he was out of earshot. "A former bodyguard betrayed him."

"Which bodyguard?" she demanded.

"René Durand."

"Durand," she whispered. In spite of his impeccable résumé, Isabelle had never liked the man. She'd tried to convince herself that his hard, cynical eyes were normal for a bodyguard, and that she had no reason to feel uneasy. She'd allowed him to be hired as one of Alexander's *carabiniers*. Her mistake.

"I should have turned him in to the police," she said fiercely.

"He's done this before?"

"Two months ago I caught him stealing a Monet from the palace—brazenly carting it out the back door as if he owned it. He gave me all kinds of excuses and pleaded with me to give him the benefit of the doubt. So I let him go."

"Well, there can be no doubt now," Paolo said. "I found him writing a ransom note. He's deeply in debt and has a grudge against you. If you want my advice, Durand should be put in solitary confinement. Or better yet—" he watched her from beneath heavily lidded eyes "—just have him disappear altogether."

"What?" she gasped.

"As the old saying goes, dead men tell no tales."

"No!"

"You said you wanted secrecy…"

A moment before she'd been ready to kill René Durand with her own bare hands, but the idea of Paolo making him "disappear" sent a chill over her body.

"Not that way," she said sharply.

For a moment he looked at her in the moonlight. His face was hidden by shadow as he said quietly, "You're taking a risk, Isabelle. Being civilized can be a weakness. He hates you. If he ever gets the chance, he might try and hurt you or the child."

She drew back. "We will be fine. Just give him to the captain of the *carabiniers*."

He clenched his jaw. "You're making a mistake."

"Fortunately, after tomorrow I'll no longer be your responsibility. Magnus—"

"Magnus will protect you?" The hard angles of Paolo's face were edged with a translucent silver light as he gave a derisive snort. "If you believe he could protect anyone from anything, love must have truly made you blind."

"I—"

"He has money to hire bodyguards, of course. And, as you pointed out, he's the tenth richest man in the world," he said coldly. "So of course you love him. Let me be the first to wish you joy."

She opened her mouth to say she didn't love

Magnus. Then closed it again. Admitting she didn't love him would just make her a bigger target for Paolo's scorn. She already had enough of a bull's-eye on her back for his pointed barbs.

"Thank you," she said over the lump in her throat. "I can't wait to be his wife."

"I'm sure you'll be very happy together, Princess."

The ice in his voice made her shiver. This was the man she had to spend the night with—share her body with? This ruthless, unfeeling man?

What had happened to the boy she'd once loved?

He was just an illusion.

Paolo would never believe that she didn't care about Magnus's money beyond how it would help her country. But the Prince came from a good family, he was kind, and—let's face it— she had to marry someone. She was nearly twenty-nine, and as her mother and counselors had so often reminded her, her duty required that she take a husband.

And Isabelle did long to have children of her own.

The fact that she didn't love the Prince, far from being a problem, was a huge bonus. It meant he could never hurt her. The one time she'd fallen in love it had caused her only grief. She'd been foolish to disregard her mother's example. Selfish to follow her heart. And she'd nearly disgraced her whole country because of it.

It was best to avoid having feelings altogether.

But there was no point in trying to explain that to Paolo. He seemed determined to hate her. He would never understand anyway. How could he, when he'd never loved anyone but himself?

She wished she'd never made such a devil's bargain. She wished she could stay at the palace and spend the warm spring day with Alexander, planning his upcoming coronation, helping him teach his little dog Jacquetta to do tricks. Making sure that he still remembered how to play. Making sure he always remembered he was loved.

Instead, she had to leave and give herself to Paolo Caretti—the only man who'd ever taken her body, the only man who'd ever taken her heart.

Isabelle shivered. His dark power was almost frightening. The people of San Piedro still slept, unaware that a coup had been prevented. What could possibly stop a ruthless billionaire with his own private army? He had no morals at all. It was why she'd known that she couldn't marry him. Known he couldn't be the father to her children…

"You can spend the rest of tonight at the palace," Paolo told her now, coldly turning away. "Tomorrow I will return to collect on our bargain."

"Tomorrow?" Her nerves couldn't wait that long! "Why not now?"

Clenching his jaw, he turned back to face her.

"Whatever the rumors say, I'm not a heartless monster. I'll allow you to spend some time with your nephew."

She wanted to be with Alexander more than anything, but her promise to Paolo was hanging over her head like an execution. Knowing she had to give herself to him, she was filled with dread…and anticipation. She wanted to get it over with so she could return to her calm, passionless life. A life that made sense. A life without passion—without pain.

She took a deep breath.

"I owe you a debt. I want to pay it." Before anyone—Magnus, the paparazzi, her mother— discovered their liaison, she wanted Paolo Caretti permanently out of her life. It was her only hope. Because he was too smart not to see what was right in front of his eyes. Sooner or later he'd figure it out. She couldn't let that happen. Not now. Not after everything she'd sacrificed.

"I'll go with you now," she said quickly. "Take me to…to…" She tried to think of someplace close to the palace, but not too close. "To your villa."

His eyebrows rose. "You know about San Cerini?"

"Of course I do." Since he'd purchased the property three years ago, she'd often watched the villa's lights across the bay. Wondering if he was there. Wondering if he was alone.

And knowing he wasn't. Paolo Caretti's list of conquests—mostly models and actresses, with a few heiresses tossed in for good measure—was legendary around the world. Something like pain went through her every time she thought about it. She told herself it was just because she pitied the woman he would someday take as his wife. If his wife loved him, she would never know a moment without heartbreak.

"Fine," he growled. "My villa. Tomorrow."

"No." She raised her chin stubbornly. "Tonight."

Moonlight cascaded over his handsome face, shadowing the chiseled lines of his cheekbones and Roman profile. "Do you really want to fight me, Isabelle? You know you'll lose."

How dared he order her around as if she were his slave? His arrogance infuriated her.

"I'm not one of your little tarts," she said haughtily. "I have responsibilities. One night, that was our bargain. So let's just go get it over with, shall we?" She made a show of glancing at her watch. "We'll have to hurry, if you please. I need to get back to the palace by 6:00 a.m. I have appointments—"

"Get it over with?" He pushed her against the rough branches of the hedge. "Get it over with? We could consummate our bargain right here. Would that be convenient enough for you?"

The hedge was sharp, full of branches stabbing into her back. She could feel his anger like a riptide, threatening to pull her under, threatening to drown her.

She'd been furious with him, and before that she'd felt hurt, but now, for the first time, she felt afraid. All the rumors she'd heard came crashing through her mind: that for all his sophistication and good-looks, Paolo Caretti was nothing more than a thug in an expensive suit. That he crushed people without remorse, taking everything he wanted—both in business and in bed.

Pushing aside her fear, she lifted her chin. "Let me go."

He grasped her hip, pressing his leg between her own. "I could just wrap your legs around me and take you here. Is that what you want, Isabelle?"

"You're hurting me!"

Abruptly, he released her.

"There is no question of getting our affair *over with,*" he said scornfully. "You are mine when I want you. That was the bargain. To take whenever and however I please."

"Just—just for one night," she stammered, hating how weak she was against his strength.

"Yes. One night." His eyes were dark and mesmerizing. Even without him touching her, she could feel it up and down her body. "Not for a half-night, sandwiched between a rescue and your morning appointments."

"But I—"

"Tomorrow morning you will be waiting for me at the back entrance of the palace. At ten o'clock." He gave her a coldly measuring appraisal that caused her cheeks to burn. "And you won't wear a rumpled suit that has gone back and forth across the Atlantic. You will wear a sexy dress and your hair down. You will do everything you possibly can to please me."

"You really are an insufferable bastard," she whispered, yearning to slap his handsome, arrogant face.

"I know what I am." Leaning forward, he stroked her cheek with a tenderness belied by the hard look in his eyes. He gave her a sensual, predatory smile. "Now, go get some rest. You're going to need it."

CHAPTER THREE

PAOLO was ten minutes late the next morning, when he pulled up behind the stables in a cherry-red Ferrari.

Furious, Isabelle bent to look at him through the open passenger window of the ultra-flashy car. "This is your idea of being discreet?"

He shrugged. Leaning across the gearshift, he lazily pushed open her door. "Get in."

For a split second Isabelle hesitated, longing to slam the door back in his face. But she couldn't do that. It wouldn't suit her plan.

Careful with the short hemline of her dress— she didn't want to reveal too much, not yet—

she climbed down into the leather seat, placing her overnight bag in her lap. "You're late."

"And you're beautiful. I'm surprised."

"What do you mean by that?"

He gave her a sharp, glinty grin. "Let's just say I didn't expect you to follow my orders so well."

He'd demanded that she try to please him, so naturally her first desire had been to take a mudbath in the nearest pigsty, but, grinding her teeth, she'd put her simmering anger aside and done her best to obey. She wore a red silk dress with a low-cut bodice and spaghetti straps, while her high-heeled espadrilles showed off her brand-new pedicure. Her long brown hair cascaded in big curls down her bare shoulders, and her lipstick and mascara were expertly applied, courtesy of her stylist. She usually hired him only for royal functions, but today she felt no guilt at the expense.

Her one-night stand with Paolo was as important as anything she'd ever done for her country. Perhaps *the* most important thing.

Paolo, on the other hand, was wearing faded jeans and an old white T-shirt so tight it showed every ridge of his hard-muscled torso.

"You look nice, too," she said ironically.

"I don't have to dress up for you." His hands turned the steering wheel with casual confidence as he pressed on the gas, speeding the Ferrari through the palace's back gate with a loud roar. He gunned down the cobblestoned hilly streets of the town, attracting startled stares from tourists returning from the flower market in the old square.

She flinched, hunching in her seat and covering her face with her hand.

"You're doing this to annoy me," she said through clenched teeth.

He lifted a dark eyebrow. "I am bowing to your wishes, *Princess*, and getting us out of San Piedro as quickly as possible."

"Stop calling me Princess."

"Isn't that your title?"

"You say it with a sneer. I don't like it. Please stop."

"As you wish, Your Serene Highness."

She flinched. Arguing with him only made things worse. She turned away as they drove along the coastal road. Looking out the window, she felt her heart start to rise in spite of everything. She was done with London's stifling economic summit, done with New York's gray sleet. Alexander was safe, she was home, and it was spring. Through her open window she could smell the seasalt and fresh air. Far beneath the cliffs she could see the blue waves of the Mediterranean sparkling in the morning light.

Paolo's villa, San Cerini, was directly across from the palace, on the other side of San Piedro Bay; traveling by speedboat it would have taken no time at all, but traveling the circuitous route by land took longer. Isabelle had taken the road many times. Magnus's family, like all the best families of Europe, also had a villa on this exclusive stretch of coastline…

Paolo's lips turned downward as they went past the von Trondhem gate. He pressed down on the gas, speeding the Ferrari faster along the curves of the cliff.

Isabelle gripped the leather edges of her seat, feeling as if any moment they might skid off the edge and plummet into the water pounding the rocks below.

He glanced at her out the corner of his eye. "Am I going too fast?"

"No," she said tensely. She'd be damned if she'd ask him to slow down. He'd frightened her in the garden last night, but she'd sworn to herself that it would be the last time she would ever let Paolo affect her. She leaned back against her black leather seat, taking a deep breath as the wind whipped through her hair. "The sooner I'm in your bed, the better."

He pushed down on the gas pedal. "I couldn't agree more."

Seconds later Paolo was driving his Ferrari down the *allée* of palm trees to his villa. With a careless wave at the guard, he went through the gate. The circular driveway went around an enormous fountain of carved stone. She looked up at the statue in amazement.

"Do you like it?" Paolo said. "The carving is from an old Russian fairy tale. This villa was built over a hundred years ago by a St. Petersburg émigré richer than half the world."

It was monstrous. A fierce firebird three times taller than a man rose triumphant from a stone sea, clutching a dying sea dragon in its vicious claws. The firebird's fierce power reminded her of the fountain's owner. Would Paolo crush her, too? She stared at it, licking her lips.

Then she saw he'd been watching her. Purposefully, she settled back against the car seat, doing her best to exude nonchalance and boredom. "A monster is your villa's mascot? Appropriate."

He abruptly stopped the car and got out. Servants immediately appeared, but to Isabelle's surprise he glowered them back.

He wrenched open her door himself. "This way, Princess."

In spite of all her proud defiance she was afraid. She was now entering his demesne—under his complete control. Feeling like a doomed French aristocrat on her way to the guillotine, Isabelle closed her eyes, relishing the sun's warmth on her skin for one last time. She had the sudden impulse to flee, to fling herself into the driver's seat and use the keys hanging in the ignition to drive the Ferrari far, far away—to a place where she'd never see Paolo again. To a place where she could forget he even existed, forget the hot kisses that had seared her with fire.

But she knew, to the depths of her soul, that no such place existed.

"Perhaps you'd like me to carry you?"

The threat of him flinging her over his shoulder like a sack of potatoes was enough to make her immediately hand him her overnight bag. He slung it over his shoulder, but still waited for her with his other hand outstretched.

With a deep breath, she placed her hand in his own.

Instantly she regretted it. A current of electricity went through her at his touch. His fingers tightened, intertwining with hers, and his eyes glittered at her with dark, sensual promise. She knew they would be in bed together long before the sun set.

Good, she told herself. Her plan was working.

But the nervous butterflies in her belly had nothing to do with any plan. She was attracted to him so much that it terrified her. She feared he was too strong for her. It would be too easy to succumb to his power. Almost impossible to resist…

With servants trailing in their wake, Paolo led her through the front door. It was strange for her to finally see the inside of the famous San Cerini. First built by the Russian nobleman in the nineteenth century, Paolo had had it expanded and rebuilt to the security of a fortress—and the luxury of a palace far more lavish than anything Isabelle knew at home.

She'd spent many hours, lonely in her bedroom, watching the lights of San Cerini across the water. Wondering which actress or heiress or artist's model he was entertaining that night. And tonight she would be the one in his bed. She would be the one to glory in his touch, to be ignited by his caress.

She could only pray that as she surrendered her body in his bed she would somehow have the strength to keep both her secret and her heart guarded…

After giving orders to a matronly housekeeper, Paolo turned back to her. "Come with me."

Isabelle allowed him to draw her through the spacious high-ceilinged rooms and up the sweeping marble stairs. She allowed him? There was a laugh! As if she had any choice in the matter! Who could stop Paolo Caretti from doing anything he wished?

Especially since her own traitorous body yearned to obey his every command...

She stopped in the doorway of his bedroom.

Thrilled.

Terrified.

My plan, she reminded herself as her body shook with conflicting emotions. *Stick to the plan.* She had to convince him to seduce her as quickly as possible. She would keep her heart frozen, layered in impenetrable frost. Then she would leave and make sure their paths never crossed again. As simple as that.

Or perhaps not so simple. Paolo picked her up from the doorway, sweeping her in his arms as if she weighed nothing.

"What—what are you doing?" she gasped.

His dark eyes looked down at her. "Carrying you over my threshold."

"But I'm not your bride!"

"You agreed to marry me once," he said softly. "Do you remember?"

A shiver raked through her. His enormous suite, overlooking San Piedro Bay in one direction and the Mediterranean Sea in the other, was the perfect setting for any honeymoon. The bedroom had high, plastered ceilings, exquisite tapestries, Louis XV furniture. Through the wide windows she could see a stone balcony overlooking the sea, and palm trees swaying in the fresh spring breeze.

It was perfect in every way—except Paolo Caretti wasn't the man she was supposed to marry. Within months she would be Prince Magnus's bride, and for the rest of her life it would be easy to keep her heart hidden and cold.

She blinked hard, willing away incomprehensible tears.

Paolo kissed her shoulder, trailing his fingers along her collarbone. Then he drew back, looking into her eyes. "Are you crying, *bella*? Is this truly so distasteful to you?"

"No," she whispered. And that was the problem. She sucked in her breath as she felt him stroke the bare skin of her back. "You can have any woman you want in the whole world," she said. "Why me? Who am I to you?"

He pushed her back against his bed, and for one intense instant the mockery disappeared from his eyes.

"You're the one who got away," he said softly.

She couldn't hide the shiver that went through her as he kissed her neck, running his hands up and down her body through the red silk. She gasped as his weight pushed her into the soft mattress. Caressing her everywhere, suckling the tender flesh of her ear, he spread her legs beneath him. Only their clothes separated them.

He had to be almost twice her weight, but

every hard pound of him felt like pure pleasure against her. His body was so muscular, so heavy, so fine. She wanted to pull off his shirt and caress his naked skin. To plunder his mouth in a hot, hard kiss.

But she didn't move. She couldn't. Except for that hot summer in New York, she'd spent her whole life following the rules and being good. No matter how she wanted to live dangerously…

He kissed her. His tongue teased hers as he reached for the bodice of her halter dress, caressing her breasts through the fabric. At the hard demand of his lips on her own, desire pounded through her blood. His kiss ignited her body. He made her feel things she did not want to feel, drugging her senses. He made her whole body tremble.

It was as if she'd been sleeping for ten years and now, suddenly, she was awake.

Somehow, her arms reached for him of their own accord. She pulled him against her, relishing the warmth of his hard, muscular chest through his cotton T-shirt. She felt everything and everywhere he touched. She felt far too much.

His hands reached beneath the silk to cup her breasts, squeezing her tight nipples between his rough fingertips. Grasping her backside, he thrust her hips upwards, moving his hips between her legs. She tried to remain still, then realized she was already swaying against him, desperate to be closer, desperate to feel him naked inside her.

As if he'd read her mind, he pulled up her dress. She could feel the silk moving up her thighs with agonizing slowness, the slippery fabric caressing her skin like water.

"Bella," he said in a low voice. *"Sì.* You are so beautiful…"

Reaching beneath her lace panties, he softly stroked her. She gasped aloud, arching her back against his fingers.

Lowering himself on the bed, he moved his head between her legs. She had the sudden realization of what he meant to do. She tried to pull back—she couldn't possibly allow—

Pushing the panties aside, he tasted her. When she tried to buck her hips away, he held her firmly in place, tempting her to accept the pleasure. Her head fell backward as he teased her with his mouth. He licked with light brushing strokes, then pressed harder, deeper, spreading her wide with the full roughness of his tongue. He tantalized her, pushing his tongue deep inside her as his finger swirled softly over her slippery, sensitive nub. His tongue and his hand switched places and he pushed a thick finger inside her, sucking and licking until she was dripping wet. He pushed in another finger, stretching her. He added a third, and she gasped. The pleasure was so great she thought she might die.

She gave a soft, soundless cry as her whole

body tightened and exploded. He paused. But he didn't stop. And before she understood what was happening she felt the pleasure start to gather tension through her body again, like dark clouds in a storm…

She whimpered. She couldn't take much more. But she didn't want his fingers. She wanted…

Breathlessly, she grabbed a belt loop of his jeans. She couldn't say what she wanted—she couldn't even think of the words—but her meaning was plain.

He stopped, looking down at her with a strange expression in his eyes. "You are mine, Isabelle. For always."

His growl cut through her sensual haze. No matter how lost she was in pleasure, the risk of what they were doing was still too terrifying to think about. "For one night," she panted. "Your mistress for one night."

"No," he said in a low voice. "For always."

He abruptly let her go.

Still spread wide across his sheets, she stared in bewildered shock as he got off the bed, leaving her bereft and vulnerable.

"What is it? Why did you stop?"

He looked down at her. "That's enough. For now."

She actually considered begging him to return to bed. So much for being made of ice! She sat up, her cheeks hot with shame. He obviously meant to prolong his torture until she would do or say anything he wished. And that was what frightened her most. She had to get this over with *now*—before she felt anything more. Before she became so intoxicated by forbidden emotions and pleasures that she'd give away everything she held dear...

She took a deep breath and forced herself to do the unthinkable.

Plan B.

"No," she said.

His eyebrows lifted. "No?"

"We're not going to wait." She stood up from the bed. Her hands shook as she untied the halter behind her back. "You're going to take me here. On this bed. Right now."

Unzipping her red dress, she let it drop to her feet. Wearing only her translucent lace bra and panties, it took all of her courage to meet his eyes.

The arrogant billionaire who had power over half the world looked as if he were suddenly having trouble breathing.

Encouraged, she stepped out of the dress, leaving it crumpled on the floor. The bra was made of deep blue silk lace, edged with ribbon and utterly see-through; the thong panties were tied with ribbon bows on each side and could be pulled off her hips with one tug. She bent to unlace her espadrilles, giving him a good view of her breasts, already clearly on view through the flimsy triangles of silk lace. Slowly, lingeringly, she pulled the sandals off her feet, tossing them aside like a stripper she'd once seen in an American movie.

"Where did you learn to do that?" he muttered.

She looked at him, praying he wouldn't see how inexperienced she felt, how totally out of her league. He'd been with so many women—would he sneer at her efforts? Or—worse—laugh? She swallowed, then, meeting his eyes, raised her chin defiantly.

"It's only morning. I'm not going to stay all day and then give you my night as well. A bargain is a bargain. Take me all day." She leaned defiantly on her tilted hip. "Tonight I'm going home."

Part of her was amazed at her own brazen behavior. But she wanted him to take her hard and fast, before she completely lost her reason. Before her heart started to remember the desperate way she'd once loved him.

And, most of all, before he discovered her secret: nine years ago she'd had his baby.

Alexander was their son.

"Please," she whispered. "Just let me return home to the people I love."

He wrenched his gaze up from her breasts.

"Nice try," he said evenly. "But you're not going anywhere."

Let me return home to the people I love.

Her words hit Paolo like a fierce mistral wind, smothering the warmth of the spring sun.

He'd meant to coldly lure her into a short-term affair—just long enough to satisfy him and leave her wanting more. True, she'd left him once, but he'd been barely more than a boy then. Much had changed. *He* had changed.

He'd arrogantly assumed that Isabelle, like every other woman, would melt like butter in his experienced hands. Instead, as he'd felt her arms twine around him on the bed, pulling him into a sweetness even sharper than he remembered, he'd been the one who started to fall.

He'd felt a tremor go through his body—a shock of desire such as he'd never known. Her kiss had sent him reeling like an untried boy. One moment in her arms, against the warmth of her skin, had sent him back in time; one hot caress and he'd forgotten all the other women he'd ever had. God help him, but he'd actually had the momentary delusion of wanting Isabelle as his wife.

He was glad she'd reminded him about Magnus.

Paolo's jaw clenched as he looked at her. Half-naked. Impossibly beautiful.

And totally in love with another man. A weak-chinned, entitled-since-birth, *civilized* prince. But why should he be surprised? She wasn't the first woman who'd chosen Magnus over him…

"Kiss me," Isabelle whispered now, putting her arms around him.

She was so petite, so soft. He felt her full breasts pushing up against his chest, her hip rubbing against his thigh. His whole body was aching for her. Painfully. As if he'd been hard for a decade, wanting her…

She leaned forward, stroking his chest.

He'd thought he could control his desire for her. He was accustomed to controlling everything—well, except the ability to sleep, damn it. But looking at her now, so seductive and powerful, in nothing more than a few scraps of flimsy lace, he wanted her almost more than he could bear.

While *she* wanted to hurry through their bargain. She wanted to marry someone else, give *him* children, give *him* all her tomorrows.

No.

One night of pleasure was suddenly not enough for Paolo. Not nearly enough.

Isabelle was meant to belong to him and no other man.

"Paolo?"

He looked down at her, feeling her tremble

beneath him like a fragile bird. "We made a bargain. One night. Not a day. Not a throwaway quickie. One full night." His lip curled. "So you'll just have to wait. Both you and that precious fiancé of yours."

"You can't keep me here—"

"I can." Picking the red dress up off the floor, he tossed it at her. "Put this back on. It's bright daylight and the windows are wide open. You look like a *puttana*."

He had a brief image of her face blanching with humiliation as he turned from her. He pushed aside his stab of regret. He knew she didn't deserve that insult. Her fire was what he'd always loved the most about her: she was sweet innocence wrapped in sin.

But the innocence was a lie. He'd learned that the hard way. It was just how she lured men into loving her—before she crushed them beneath the weight of her scorn.

Clenching his jaw, he turned away.

"Where are you going?" she whispered, holding the red dress in her arms like a scarlet slash against her pale belly.

Without answering, he stalked out the door and down the hall toward his study. He disliked his bedroom anyway. The room was a cage—the place where he hadn't had a decent night's sleep since he'd bought San Cerini. His insomnia had started here. But it hadn't stayed here. It now followed him everywhere: his New York penthouse, his Irish estate. He'd exercised until he dropped. Boxed in a fight club till he was covered with blood. Even made love to anonymous women for hours on end. Nothing had helped.

So? he told himself harshly. Insomnia just gave him more time to work. In the last three years his net worth had quadrupled. His global holdings—comprising steel factories and metal commodities trading, as well as the famous Caretti Motors—had turned him into a billionaire. He now had everything any man could want.

And if surviving on three hours of sleep a night made him abrupt and rude at times—well, people knew not to test him. His employees knew to get it right the first time.

Paolo pushed the door open to his study. His bookshelves included everything from a biography of Glenn Curtiss to a paperback history of nitrous oxide; his sleek black desk had a view overlooking the bay. When he was at San Cerini he was nearly always here, or in his ten-car garage, tinkering with engines. Engines calmed him. Engines made sense. If he took care of them, they took care of him.

Unlike people.

Damn it, he'd asked her to marry him.

He grabbed a bottle of expensive Scotch from the cabinet. The night before she'd planned to leave New York for the summer, he'd looked down at her, sleeping in his arms. "Marry me," he'd whispered, never expecting that she would.

But she'd opened those beautiful eyes and

said, in a trembling voice, "Yes." Joy had washed over him such as he'd never known. They'd slept all night in a lovers' embrace on his tiny worn mattress on the floor.

The next day, while she'd been at Barnard, packing up her room, he'd sold his only possession of value—the old engine he'd been tinkering with for a year—and traded it for an engagement ring. Determined to propose properly, he'd used his landlady's kitchen to prepare fettuccine from his grandmother's old recipe. Setting up a card table at the center of his studio apartment, he'd covered it with borrowed linen and mismatched dishware, crowning the table with a centerpiece of a candle in an old wine bottle.

But somehow, in spite of all his care, everything had fallen apart. Isabelle had been nervous and distracted over dinner, barely eating two bites of pasta. And when he'd finally knelt on one knee before her, holding out the precious ring and asking her to be his wife, she'd changed in front of his eyes.

Snatching the engagement ring from his out-stretched hand, she'd stared at the tiny diamond in disbelief. "My *husband*? Are you out of your *mind*?" She had barked a laugh, then tossed the ring back scornfully into his face. "I've just been slumming with you, Paolo—having a bit of fun. I assumed you knew that. Marriage? I'm Princess of San Piedro. You're nobody."

Paolo poured himself a double Scotch, staring through the wide windows toward the palace across the bay. The same view he'd brooded over his very first night in the villa, watching the lights of the *palais* shimmer across the dark water.

Love made a man deaf, dumb and blind.

But he should thank her, really. The engage-ment ring had bought back his engine—the eventual prototype of the Caretti motorcycle engine—and her scorn had spurred him into becoming richer and more powerful than he'd ever imagined. And, though he'd been ruthless at times, he'd never sunk to his father's level. He'd made his fortune with no help from the old neighborhood.

The only time he'd ever used those connections was this past week—at Isabelle's request—to find her nephew.

But he saw now that, no matter what he did, she would always see him as a lowlife. No matter how many billions he had in his bank account, his net worth would always be zero to her.

He took a long drink of the single-malt Scotch, draining the crystal glass to the dregs. He could handle it. He didn't care what people thought of him—now. As a child it hadn't been so easy. His father had been constantly in and out of jail…his mother had abandoned him when he was three months old. Alone, he'd been an easy target. But by the time he'd been in fifth grade he'd learned how to start a fight, how to launch himself at opponents far bigger than he was and make them take back their words. It had been a valuable experience. It had made him stronger.

But that didn't mean he wanted his own children to endure the same.

He wanted to give his future children a blood-line so exalted that, coupled with his wealth, they would always be treated well. Give them a mother who would love them enough to stay…

Suddenly his eyes narrowed. Too good to be his mistress, was she? Too good to marry him?

I'm Princess of San Piedro. You're nobody.

"Signor Caretti, is everything all right?"

An anxious servant stood in the open doorway of his study.

"*Sì.*" A cruel smile curved his lips. "Everything is fine."

He would show her. He'd lure her. Caress her. Woo her. Make her laugh. Make her love him. And most of all…

"Your new motorcycle has arrived, *signore,*"

the young man said. "It is waiting in the garage. Signor Bertolli is already checking it over."

"Excellent." Paolo rose from his desk. As he went down the sweeping stairs towards his ten-car garage, he'd already come to a decision.

If Isabelle wouldn't willingly give him her respect, he would just take it. He would *own* the most famous princess in the world, possess her completely.

He would seduce her. Get her pregnant.

Paolo would force her to become his wife.

CHAPTER FOUR

AFTER he'd left the bedroom, Isabelle stumbled backward, sinking onto the high mattress. She curled up in a ball, clutching the noxious red dress against her belly. A warm breeze, sweet with spring honeysuckle and sharp with the salty tang of the sea, swayed the curtains as she stared out blindly through the wide windows.

The memory of the way she'd stripped in front of him, demanding that he make love to her, replayed in her mind. She—a princess of San Piedro, a scion of the proud de Luceran bloodline—had debased herself to the man she feared and despised. And all she'd gotten for her trouble was his rejection.

The only man she'd ever loved, the father of her child, had just called her a *whore*.

"Oh." She gasped aloud from shame, covering her face with her hands. But even with her eyes closed she could still see the curl of his lip, still hear his scornful words. She'd have willingly jumped off the balcony and let herself be swallowed by the sea if it had meant she'd never have to face him again.

But she was Princess of San Piedro. Her country needed her. Her son needed her. Shamed or not, she had to go on. Get up. Get it over with.

With a deep breath, she forced herself to open her eyes. Slowly she straightened her spine, unfolding her body. She rose from the bed, still wearing only her lace bra and panties. Then she stared down at the expensive bit of red silk crumpled up in her hand. Her eyes narrowed with hatred.

She stalked across the priceless Savonnerie carpet to the Louis XV marble fireplace.

Tossing the dress into the fireplace, she took a match from a nearby wrought-iron log rack. Lighting the match, she lit the expensive red dress on fire and watched it burn.

It was finished.

She would die before she tried to seduce Paolo again.

When there was nothing but ash left, Isabelle turned on her heel. She briefly hesitated when she saw a plush white robe hanging from the bathroom door, then grabbed it. Wrapping her body in his robe, she rang the bell.

A few moments later his housekeeper appeared. She had rosy cheeks, and salt-and-pepper hair pulled back into a bun.

She looked at Isabelle with critical eyes before she lowered her gaze with a brief curtsy.

No doubt the woman was thinking the same thing that Paolo had said: she was nothing better than a harlot. Her cheeks went hot, but she raised her chin, staring the housekeeper down. "I am Isabelle de Luceran."

"Ne sono, Principessa. I am Signora Bertolli."

"Somewhere in this heap of bricks is my overnight bag. Please find it for me."

"Sì, immediatemente."

A few minutes later, she reappeared with the overnight bag. "Shall I unpack for you, *Principessa*?" Not waiting for an answer, she opened the bag. "Ah, such beautiful clothes," she said wistfully.

Looking at her, Isabelle felt some envy of her own. Signora Bertolli likely had a snug little cottage, a husband to take her to the movies. Children. Family dinners. Conversations in the kitchen. Everything Isabelle had once dreamed of.

Everything she'd once thought she would have with Paolo.

The day after he'd first proposed in bed she'd gone back to her dorm, still reeling at her decision. She knew her family would never accept him as her husband, and neither would her people, but she didn't care. She was ready to defy them all.

She had found her mother's bodyguards outside her door, and Queen Clothilde sitting stiffly on her unmade bed. Praying she'd convince her mother to accept the match, Isabelle had told her about the engagement.

"To a poor mechanic?" her mother had gasped in horror.

"I love him, *Maman*."

Her mother had shaken her head.

"Love." She'd spat out the word bitterly. "Men are not faithful, *ma fille*. If you marry for love you will have a lifetime of heartbreak. This man has no family, no fortune. And do you think this...*nobody* would actually enjoy marriage to you? Sacrificing his own desires? Living entirely for others? Always being criti-cized and watched without the slightest bit of personal freedom? He would be mocked and scorned… Isabelle—look at me when I'm talking to you. *Isabelle*!"

She'd sunk dizzily to the bed. At the time she'd thought it was just the sensation of her heart breaking. She'd forced herself to sit quietly as her mother proved why it would be best for everyone, including Paolo, if Isabelle ended the affair. Ignoring her body's warnings, she'd finally, tearfully, agreed.

She'd gone to Paolo's apartment for dinner and crushed his hopes with the words her mother had suggested—coldly, cruelly, making sure he'd never miss her.

She'd known it was the right thing to do. He'd deserved far better than a life with her. But still it had nearly killed her.

An hour later, as they had prepared to leave for San Piedro, Isabelle's dizzy spells had abruptly intensified. The Queen's doctor had examined Isabelle on the private plane. They'd soon discovered that, at the tender age of eighteen, she was leaving New York with far more than just a broken heart…

"Will you be staying for long, *Principessa*?"

Signora Bertolli's question brought Isabelle back to the present. "No. I intend to leave tonight. Stop unpacking, please. Just leave the bag with me."

The woman gave a dignified nod and turned to go.

"Wait."

She halted, looking back at her. *"Sì, Principessa?"*

"Do you know where I might find Signor Caretti?"

"I believe he's in the garage. Shall I take you there?"

Her jaw hardened. "I'll find him."

Minutes later Isabelle was dressed in prim white underwear, a pale pink cashmere sweater set, her grandmother's pearls and a demure knee-length skirt. Her quilted leather handbag bounced against her hip as she stalked across the villa, crossing the garden in her beige peeptoe pumps.

When she saw Paolo she would be cold. Bitingly polite. She would cut him down in the most ladylike way. She would force him to realize he could not insult her and keep her prisoner.

She would not stay here.

She had a child to raise and a man to marry... One out of love, the other out of duty.

Paolo, she would say, *I made a good-faith effort, which you refused. I therefore consider myself absolved of our agreement...*

She heard Paolo's voice ahead, speaking in Italian.

And, furthermore, you can go to hell. Although of course she wouldn't say that last bit. Repressing her own feelings for the sake of diplomacy had been drummed into her since birth. But Paolo had a way of making her hot all over, causing her to lose her reserve. She hated that. A princess always had to stay in control. She certainly never swore at a man in public, no matter how richly he might deserve it…

She saw Paolo and stopped dead in her tracks.

He was standing at one of the open garage doors, kneeling in front of an old upside-down motorcycle with a large single-cut file in his hand. Next to him, a boy about Alexander's age peered into the engine.

"Look at the casing now," Paolo said.

The boy looked. "It's so much better! I thought those old bits of gasket were stuck on there for good!"

"Not with the right file," Paolo said, his voice strong with approval and affection. "See how easily twenty years can be stripped away?"

"Are you bothering Signor Caretti, Adriano?" Bertolli called from the back of the garage.

"No, I'm helping," the boy replied, then turned anxiously to Paolo. "I *am* helping, *sì*?"

"You're a great help, Adriano," Paolo told him. "I couldn't do without you, *giovannato*."

Isabelle started in shock at the warmth in his voice.

"So hire me on your pit crew," the boy pleaded. "I swear you won't regret it!"

"Adriano," his father said warningly.

"I'm sure I wouldn't regret it." Paolo ruffled the boy's hair. "You have skill and promise."

"So you agree—?"

"When you're older I will be glad to hire you, if you still wish it. But for now—school!"

"Oh, school," he replied, with good-natured grumbling.

Watching them from the shadows of the juniper trees, Isabelle felt her knees tremble beneath her.

This was the man she'd kept from his son. The man she'd told herself had no business being a father. Watching him smile down at the boy, she felt a wave of guilt crash over her. Guilt that threatened to drown her.

She tried to fight it off with all her old justifications.

She'd had no choice, she told herself desperately. Marrying Paolo would have been a disaster. Raising a baby with him outside of marriage would have been even worse. Their child had deserved to be brought up a prince, with two loving, married parents.

But now those parents were dead, a voice whispered inside her. Didn't Alexander deserve to know that he still had a mother and father on earth?

He's mourning the only parents he's ever known. The parents he loved, she argued back fiercely. It would only confuse him to know the truth.

But—

Besides, she argued more loudly, if Paolo knew the truth he might try to get custody. No matter how wonderful he might seem with children now, she couldn't risk ruining

Alexander's life. His Kingship. She couldn't just blindly trust Paolo to do the right thing for his son, for all of them…

"Isabelle?"

She looked up. Paolo was standing by his motorcycle. Chrome and black steel gleamed in the noon sun as he smiled at her. "I'm glad you're here."

Looking at his smile, it was as if she'd gone back in time to the moment she'd first met him, when Paolo had arrived at her stalled limousine in a blue mechanic's jumpsuit, wrench gleaming like a lightning bolt in his hand. He'd made her laugh, flirting with her as if she were any college girl, and asked her to a movie. She'd relished the anonymity of the theater. Ordering popcorn and soda. Nearly dropping both when he put his arm around her.

Afterward, they'd climbed five flights of stairs to his tiny apartment. It had been at the door, beneath a single swaying lightbulb, that he'd first kissed her. Then he'd smiled, and for the first time in her life she'd understood the meaning of the words *warmth* and *home*…

Paolo's smile now was the same. It was exactly the same.

As he came toward the juniper trees his eyes were intent on her. She felt his look down to her toes. He took her hand, and his touch flooded her with warmth more vivid than sunlight.

"I'm sorry for what I said—about the dress." He softly kissed the back of her hand. "I didn't mean it."

Her eyes widened. All her years of social training hadn't prepared her for this. As far as she knew, Paolo Caretti had never apologized to anyone for anything.

"Can you forgive me?" he asked humbly.

She shook her head, trying to remember what she'd meant to say to him. All rational thought had evaporated from her mind like morning mist in sunlight. "I came to find you…to say…"

He waited patiently, but when she didn't continue he gently prompted, "There's something you wanted to say to me?"

"Yes. I… I…" She licked her lips as she stared up at him.

"Tell me, *bella*." Clasping his fingers firmly around hers, he pulled her closer. He looked down at her, their faces inches apart. "Tell me anything."

"I want to tell you…"

She tried to remember her planned insults, but, looking into his face all she could think was, *You have a son. We have a son.*

He raised an eyebrow at her. "Yes?"

But she couldn't risk Alexander's life just to make her own conscience feel better. What if Paolo told the whole world? What if he demanded custody?

What effect would it have on Alexander, on

the whole nation, if it were known that the King of San Piedro was really the illegitimate son of a corrupt Italian-American billionaire?

And what if, demanding time with their child, he stayed near Isabelle forever? Forced to spend every day beneath the assault of his dangerous charm—his smiles, his skilled lovemaking—what chance would she possibly have of survival? Even if by some miracle she forced herself to marry Magnus, how long could she keep her heart in ice?

"Isabelle?"

"I forgive you." She could barely speak the words over the guilt choking her. Forgive Paolo? She was such a fraud! Grandly forgiving him for a verbal insult when she'd done a far greater injury to him by keeping him from his child!

"Thank you." He released her hand.

Her whole body suddenly hurt. All her life she'd tried to be silent, graceful, dignified.

She'd been constantly aware of cameras rolling, people watching.

But it was still often hard to keep her emotions in check. Her family was brittle with secrets. Her mother, once so romantic, had become sharp and thin from enduring her father's endless affairs before he died. Isabelle's brother Maxim had taken a Danish princess as his wife in an arranged marriage. They'd had an amicable arrangement—until Karin had fallen in love with him and stressful years of fertility treatment had taken their toll. By the time their son was two years old, Maxim had started visiting a little house in Cannes, leaving Princess Karin as bitter and lonely as her mother-in-law.

Isabelle had promised herself that she would never endure in silence, as her mother had. She would never suffer like Karin.

She'd once thought Paolo was different from any man she'd ever known. When she'd found out she was pregnant she'd begged her mother to reconsider allowing them to marry. In addition to the scandal it would cause for Isabelle to be an unmarried mother, a child's life was now at stake. A baby needed two parents! she'd argued.

Hours after Isabelle had forced herself to fling the ring back in Paolo's face, her mother had reluctantly allowed herself to be persuaded to meet him. Isabelle still remembered how excited she'd felt, climbing those five flights of stairs. She'd felt sure her mother would accept him—how could she not love him as she did? Isabelle would marry Paolo, have his baby, and they would all be so happy…

Then she'd reached the landing.

The blond tart from next door had been silhouetted in Paolo's open doorway, wearing only a bra and shorts. In the predawn light her mussed hair and his half-naked body had made it obvious that they were kissing farewell after a night of lovemaking.

Her mother had stopped cold beside her. Before the lovers could turn around, she'd taken her daughter's hand, gently pulling her away from the scene. "Come away, *ma fille*," she'd whispered. "Come away."

Now, Paolo touched Isabelle's cheek. "I was wrong to insult you, *cara mia*," he said quietly. "You are generous to forgive my thoughtless words."

Isabelle sucked in her breath. A lifetime of secrets pressed down on her, leaving her tense enough to shatter.

"I am the one who should thank you," she managed. "For saving Alexander. I will never forget it. I will always be grateful for what you did for him. For me."

The expression in his dark gaze changed. Brushing a brown tendril from her face, he looked down at her.

"I will always protect you, Isabelle," he said in a low voice. "I protect what's mine."

"And you still think I'm yours?" she whispered.

He gave her an enigmatic smile, brief, like a sudden April shower. Mysterious. Charismatic. Powerful. "I know you are."

She had a sudden fierce longing for it to be true. That she did belong to him—not just for today, but for always. That they could go back in time and be young and naïve again. Before she'd discovered that loving Paolo—loving any man—would lead to a lifetime of anguish and heartbreak…

But there was no point in wishing. They had one day together before she married someone else. Someone safe. Someone who would never, ever break her heart or leave her crying at night.

Turning away, she cleared her throat. "I need to make a call."

"Go ahead," he said, not moving a muscle.

Pulling her phone from her Chanel handbag, she dialed the number of the captain of the

King's *carabiniers*. She spoke with the man quietly, then closed her phone.

"René Durand is in jail," she said to Paolo.

"I told you I'd take care of it."

"I needed to make sure."

"Why?" he asked evenly. "Couldn't you just trust my word?"

Trust Paolo? No. Not with her son, and not with her heart. No matter how she wished she could.

Her headache was starting to pound all the way round the back of her neck. She rubbed her forehead, blinking hard. She knew from experience that only one thing would make her feel better. Only one thing would help her forget the stress of enduring things she couldn't change.

It was an ordinary pleasure—something other people did every day—but it was a rare special treat for her. Her solace when she was desperate to forget the *princess* and the *de Luceran* in her name and be just Isabelle.

In sudden decision, she held out her hand. "Come with me."

He tilted his head. "Where?"

But even as he asked the question he put his hand in hers. And beneath the bright Mediterranean sun Isabelle gave him a smile that rose as slow and sure as the tide. "You'll see."

"Do you like it?"

Paolo could not answer her. He was afraid to move his tongue. Afraid it might make him taste more of what he had in his mouth.

"Tell me the truth," Isabelle insisted.

He looked around wildly for an escape. The outdoor terrace was warm with sunlight and surrounded by flowers beneath swaying palm trees, overlooking the jutting cliffs of San Piedro Bay.

He was tempted to jump off the balustrade and take his chances with the rocks.

"Paolo?"

He forced himself to gulp down the half-raw, half-burned egg whites mixed with undercooked asparagus. His belly lurched. He grabbed his *tazza* of scalding hot black Italian coffee, hoping that it would burn every tastebud.

But his sacrifice was all in vain. When he looked up, she was still watching him, dewy-eyed with expectation.

"I got the recipe from a book," she said with pride.

"A cookbook?" he asked faintly.

"Well, I had to modify it a little bit. I took out the hollandaise sauce and the cheese, and replaced the ham with asparagus. Do you like it?"

He looked at her. "Isabelle, I can't lie to you…"

But her face looked so vulnerable, so hungry for approval. He stopped.

His emotions had taken a turn in the last hour. He'd been coldly furious at her—until she'd surprised him with her gratitude for saving her nephew. Then she'd turned around and insulted his ability to protect her, phoning the captain to make sure that Durand was in jail. *Dio santo,* what did she think? That Paolo might have simply abandoned the kidnapper to play roulette in some Monte Carlo casino?

Then, watching her rush around the large kitchen—his soon-to-be bride and mother of his children, so damned sexy in an apron—he'd been aroused in an almost primal way. He had thoroughly relished watching her cook.

It had never occurred to him to supervise her methods. He had made his own meals from a young age—with an absent mother and a father frequently in jail it had been a necessary skill to prevent starving to death. But Isabelle had had no such advantage. She'd had a palace of servants at her beck and call, and had never learned to cook or clean. He accepted that. He'd just never imagined what evil she might create with a pan.

"It's healthy, isn't it?" Isabelle said hopefully.

"Light, but gourmet? I've been told asparagus adds a wonderful flavor and crunch."

Literally biting his lip, he managed, "I've never tasted anything like it."

Isabelle's face lit up.

"I'm so glad," she said. "It's my only real hobby. It helps me relax. I've cooked many times for the servants at the palace, but I was never sure if they really liked it or were just eating it to please me. You're the rudest person I know, so I was sure you'd tell me the truth."

Paolo suddenly felt very sorry for the whole servant class. Regular meals such as this seemed rampant cruelty. Although it was cruel to Isabelle, too, since she obviously had no idea how truly awful her cooking was. What those long-suffering servants said in private would likely have made her ears burn with horror.

"Aren't you going to finish your breakfast?"

He glanced down at his full plate with dismay.

"Shall I serve you some more?"

A shudder went through his whole body. "No."

"It's no trouble, really. I have a whole panful!"

Enough was enough. He had other ways of wooing her. Ways that were far more appetizing. Ways far more likely to get her pregnant. He didn't intend to marry her for her cooking, anyway.

Grabbing her wrist, he pulled her into the chair next to his. "Let me serve you for a change."

She shook her head shyly. "I like cooking for other people. That's the whole point. It helps me relax."

Cruel or not, it was time she learned the truth. Taking the pan, he piled several spoonfuls of the egg mixture onto an empty plate. He shoved the plate toward her, pushing a fork into her hand. "Have some."

"Really, I couldn't—"

"Eat," he ordered.

"Fine," she said with a sigh. She stabbed some

eggs and asparagus with her fork. "I suppose I am pretty hungry. It couldn't hurt to—"

She tasted it, and blanched. Gulping it down painfully, she grabbed the pan and looked down at it with consternation. She looked up at him accusingly. "It's *awful!*"

"Yes."

"Why didn't anyone tell me?"

He glanced significantly at the heavy cast-iron pan. "Perhaps they were afraid you'd resort to violence?"

She dropped the pan with a loud thunk against the table.

"Oh," she moaned, leaning forward and covering her face with her hands. "All this time my servants were eating my food—and what? Tossing it into the plants when I wasn't looking? Laughing at me behind my back?"

"Both, probably."

She shook her head, but he saw tears in her eyes. "Why couldn't they just tell me the truth? Why did they have to let me make a fool of myself?"

He looked at her. "I'll always tell you the truth. Even if it hurts."

She snorted a laugh.

"I will," he said.

She wiped her eyes. "Even Magnus lied. I cooked breakfast for him twice. He said it was delicious. He asked for more."

If she'd made Magnus breakfast it had likely been after a long night of lovemaking. The thought made Paolo want to punch something—preferably the Prince's smugly handsome face. But he couldn't really blame him for lying. Hell, even Paolo might have honestly thought her food tasted terrific after a night of making love to her.

Ten years ago he'd had no money to take Isabelle to restaurants, and she'd been afraid someone might discover their affair. They'd rarely left his apartment. He'd set up pillows on the floor for seats and heated up canned ravioli and baked beans on a hotplate. They'd eaten with plastic forks from paper plates. Not very gourmet. Not very romantic.

But somehow her company had made even those cheap meals taste delicious. Isabelle had a way of making everything taste like dessert…

He looked down at his plate ruefully. Almost everything.

"Paolo?" she said softly. "Did you really mean it? You'll never lie to me?"

Tilting his head, he watched her. "I'm planning to seduce you, get you pregnant with my child, and make you my bride."

She blinked at him for several seconds, then hiccoughed a laugh. "Very funny."

"Yes," he said. "Aren't I just?"

Rising from the table, he held out his arm. "It's noon. How about we forget breakfast and have lunch instead?"

"You're going to cook for me?" she asked,

looking up at him in surprise. "Just like the old days?"

He didn't blame her for sounding shocked. With all of her servants, all her glamour, why would she ever want to eat such a plain, cheap meal again? The thought set his teeth on edge. The bad old days. When he'd been young, broke, and stupidly in love. When they'd made love for hours, then slept all night long in each other's arms. Nights he'd never fully appreciated until now.

He pushed the thought away. He had other advantages now. And to force Isabelle to become his bride he would use them all.

"No, I'm not going to cook," he said. "I'm in no mood to open up a can, and even if I were I have people to do that for me."

She looked up at him inquisitively. "So, what did you have in mind?"

He gave her a sharp smile. "I'm thinking Italian…"

CHAPTER FIVE

AFTER his private plane had landed at the Ciampino Airport in Rome, Paolo led her down the steps to the tarmac. Isabelle stopped in her tracks when she saw the motorcycle waiting for them below.

"What's that?" she demanded.

"Our ride."

Was he trying to punish her for the way she'd nearly poisoned him that morning? She made a self-conscious motion to her hair, hanging in thick waves down her shoulders, and to her knee-length pencil skirt. "I'm not sure I can…"

"You can," he said firmly. Taking the keys from the servant standing beside the gleaming beast of a cruiser, he nodded the man's dismissal. He threw his leg over the seat and held out his hand. "Get behind me."

She stood uncertainly, biting her lip like a nervous schoolgirl.

"Surely, Princess," he mocked, "you're not frightened?"

"Of course not." Terrified was more like it. "It's just… Do you know what the traffic is like in Rome?" She gave a nervous laugh. "It doesn't have to be a Rolls-Royce, but I'd like a few inches of steel around me. Can't you phone and order a car? Or, better yet, a tank?"

"Are you questioning my driving skills?"

"No, I just—"

"Then get on," he said, still holding out his hand. And this time there was plenty of steel— in his voice.

Isabelle realized that she had two choices. She could either admit that the idea of riding a motorcycle scared her silly and refuse to go, or she could take his hand, close her eyes, and hold on tight.

Her pride made the choice for her. She strapped her Chanel purse across her chest and hiked up her slim skirt to a scandalous position at mid-thigh. Leaning on his arm, she climbed onto the motorcycle seat behind him.

He handed her a helmet. "Put this on."

He didn't need to ask her twice. Just the idea of nothing but bare skin between her and the road was enough to make her whole body tremble. He gripped the throttle and they drove off with a roar that seemed as loud as an aircraft engine.

She held him tight, pressing her body against his as they drove into the city. As their bodies leaned against every fast curve, every dangerous traffic circle, the engine vibrated between her legs. They drove down the crowded Via dei Fori Imperiali past the Colosseum, and his hard backside rubbed against the bare skin of her inner thighs. She pressed her breasts against his back as she wrapped her arms around him, holding on tight. Through the front of his cotton T-shirt she could feel the warmth of his flat, muscular belly. Wind streamed through his short dark hair, carrying the scent of clean shampoo and heady musk, and something masculine and foreign.

He wasn't wearing a helmet. Of course not. Nothing would, or could, ever hurt him. Even a crash would leave him untouched. A man like Paolo could walk through flames unscathed.

He didn't know what it was like to be afraid. Tightening her hands around him as they drove past the Piazza Venezia, she shook her head angrily. What was wrong with her? Envying first the housekeeper, and now Paolo. She had a great deal to be thankful for in her own life. Alexander was safe. Wasn't that enough?

But years of loneliness were catching up with her. Since she'd left college she'd been afraid to have close friends. Confidantes betrayed her to tabloids. Her only real friends had been Karin and Maxim, and now they both were dead. Dead on vacation in Majorca, where they'd gone on a second honeymoon, trying to revive their marriage…

Isabelle blinked back tears, missing them.

Even when they'd been alive, her days had consisted of royal duties and required social functions. She'd rarely left the palace for fun, and she'd always slept alone. Other than Magnus's brief, constrained kisses of a few weeks ago, she'd never allowed any man to touch her. Always prim and proper in public, she'd been dubbed the "ice princess" by the paparazzi, and that was pretty much on target. For ten years she'd been as frozen as Antarctica.

But beneath the constraining safety and heat of Paolo's helmet, with the dark blur of the road just inches beneath her shoes, she had the sudden yearning to feel things again. To be brave. To be free. To let consequences be damned…

Paolo pulled the motorcycle abruptly to a stop at a trattoria near the Piazza Navona. Parking the hundred-thousand euro Caretti motorcycle cross-wise in a tiny space between a Fiat and an old BMW, he reached back to help her. Encircling her waist with his hands, he gently lifted her to the sidewalk. His hands were so large his fingertips could almost touch around her.

"What are we doing here?" she asked in confusion.

He glanced back at the trattoria, and his dark eyebrows lifted sardonically. "I could be mistaken, but generally people eat at restaurants. Lunch, in this case."

He didn't seem to notice or care as strangers on the sidewalk slowed down, staring at them. Or the way people's eyes widened in sudden recognition.

"We can't eat here," she said quietly, smiling for the crowds. "Paparazzi will be on their way in seconds—if they aren't here already."

He stopped, looking down at her. "This trattoria has the very best fettuccine *alla Romana* in the world. I want you to try it."

She licked her suddenly dry lips. "But then everyone would know—"

"Know what? That you eat pasta?" His jaw hardened. "Or that you'd share a meal with a man like me?"

"I… I…" She licked her lips. It was such a small thing. And yet the prospect of taking Paolo's arm and boldly going into the trattoria, to enjoy a meal like anyone else, gave her vertigo like tottering on the edge of a cliff.

He held out his hand. "It's just fettuccine, Isabelle."

His dark eyes mesmerized her, luring her with everything she'd denied herself for the last ten years. Sensuality. Freedom. Risk.

Her cell phone started to ring. Fumbling with her handbag, she pulled out the phone and saw it was her mother's private number.

Just the thought of what her mother would say when she found out about Paolo made Isabelle's hackles rise with irritated rebellion. She tossed the phone back into the black quilted bag. Defiantly, she put her hand in his.

A slow smile spread across Paolo's face.

"*Grazie, cara mia,*" he said softly, his voice thick with approval.

It's not that hard to be reckless, she thought in surprise as he led her into the restaurant. *Not with him to guide me...*

The interior of the trattoria was small and cozy, apparently unchanged since the 1950s. A waiter came to their table and Paolo didn't bother to open his menu. "We'll have the fettuccine *alla Romana*."

"No!" Isabelle protested, desperately scanning the menu for something healthy. Allowing herself to be blackmailed into sex was one thing, but eating fattening food was another. She must be thin, as a matter of duty, and if her mother hadn't told her that the designers who sent her free clothes certainly would.

"Maybe baked fish?" she suggested weakly. "Lettuce with lemon juice?"

The waiter looked down at her with frank Italianate horror.

Paolo's expression didn't budge. "Fettuccine. For both of us," he said firmly.

He took the menu from her hand, and as his fingers brushed hers she gave in. She'd already gone into the restaurant. By tomorrow photos would be flashed around the world, of her having lunch in Rome with the ruthless billionaire motorcycle racer Paolo Caretti. Compared to that, eating a plate of pasta seemed a small sin. Why not enjoy it?

"You're too thin, anyway," he added under his breath with a wicked smile. "I intend to fatten you up, *bella*."

"Very well." She stared up at him for several heartbeats, her lips slightly parted. "Fettuccine."

"And a bottle of wine," Paolo ordered, mentioning a specific vintage that was both expensive and exceedingly rare. With a nod of appreciation the waiter disappeared, leaving them alone.

Isabelle glanced around the tiny trattoria. Every other table was filled, but other than a few surreptitious glances none of the other patrons seemed particularly interested in taking photographs or demanding autographs.

She looked at Paolo in surprise. "I think we *can* have lunch here."

"Do I really need to explain the concept of a restaurant again?"

She smothered a laugh. "No. I get it."

"Good." He gave her a heavy-lidded sensual smile. "Because I intend to satisfy your every appetite."

Her cheeks went hot. Ever since they'd left San Cerini he'd been like this: making small talk about the weather, discussing the upcoming Cannes Film Festival, sympathizing about the state of San Piedro's economy. But beneath it all his eyes were undressing her. His expression clearly said that he was picturing her in his bed.

It was an image she herself could imagine all too well. But if that was the case why had he refused her mere hours ago, when she'd been half-naked in his bedroom?

The waiter reappeared and uncorked the wine. He poured an inch into a wine glass. Paolo took a sip, then nodded his approval. The waiter filled their two large-stemmed glasses half-full of the ruby-colored wine, then placed the bottle between them on the table.

Isabelle immediately picked up her glass, hoping the cool dark wine would calm her. But instead of numbing her senses, as she'd hoped, the tannins lingered tantalizingly on her tongue, and the alcohol's warmth spread up and down her body, tingling her scalp and toes. She licked her lips, then looked up and saw him watching her from beneath heavily lidded eyes.

He was playing with her, she thought suddenly. Like a sleek panther running down his prey. And her nerves were already so frayed that she wasn't sure she could take much more of his charm.

She put down her glass with a clang. "Why are you acting like this?"

"Like what?"

"So friendly. So flirty. I don't understand. You know that I want to end our bargain. You could have me in your bed whenever you wish. Why are you acting like we're on a date? You don't need to seduce me."

His dark eyes met hers. "Perhaps I want to."

She wanted to shake her fists in frustration. "But why?"

"Am I doing it improperly?" He tilted his head as he watched her through narrowed eyes. "I suppose your lover does it quite differently."

She frowned. "My lover?"

"Prince Magnus."

She looked at him sharply. He'd said the name with a deliberate casualness belied by the hard set of his jaw. "Magnus is not my lover."

His expression didn't change. "Who's the liar now?"

"Believe what you want, but he and I have never been in bed together. We've barely even kissed."

His eyes darkened imperceptibly. "Kissed?"

She choked out a laugh. "You've got to be joking. You're critical of me kissing a man who's proposed marriage? You, who've slept with half the actresses and models in Europe?"

Leaning back in his chair, he stretched his arms behind his head, suddenly appearing much more relaxed. "I don't sleep much. A man's got to stay busy somehow."

"From everything I've heard, you're very busy indeed," she said, irritated.

He shrugged. "Work and pleasure. What else is there in life?"

"You used to believe in other things." She swallowed. "Love, for instance."

He stared at her for a moment. "That was a long time ago."

"And now?"

"I believe in hard work. I believe in honesty." His gaze lingered over her body. "I believe in protecting what's mine."

She felt his hot glance against her skin, stroking her hair, cupping her breasts, caressing her naked thighs. She took a deep breath, struggling against her desire by stoking her anger into a flame. "But you don't believe in keeping it, do you?"

"What do you mean?"

She knew she should keep her mouth shut, but a decade of rage wouldn't let her. She raised her chin. "You only want me because you think you can't have me."

His eyebrows lowered like a dark, cold storm. "We've already agreed that you're mine."

"For today. And the minutes are passing. In a few hours I'll be gone. That's just how you like it, isn't it? Keeping things nice and simple in your queue."

"What are you talking about?"

Her heart was in her throat. "You say you protect what's yours, but you don't. You like the pursuit, but once you possess something it loses its value. The last time we had fettuccine—"

"I don't want to talk about it," he bit out.

"You asked me to marry you." She felt tears behind her eyes, and angrily blinked them away. She would die before Paolo Caretti saw her cry again. "You swore that you loved me. You begged me to run away with you."

"And as I recall," he said acidly, "you tossed the ring back in my face. Let's not talk about the past. I find it all very boring."

"You promised me forever, but within hours you replaced me with the blond tart next door!"

"How do you know?" he demanded.

"Because I saw her!" she cried. "The next morning I saw you kissing her!"

He narrowed his eyes. "You came back to the apartment? Why? Did you have a sudden urge for more *slumming*?"

She sucked in her breath, hurting to remember the cold phrases her mother had given her, the words she'd thought she had to use to make Paolo let her go.

"Damn you," she whispered. "I loved you. But you couldn't even be faithful to me for a single night."

He took a drink of wine, then set the glass down.

"You gave me no reason to be."

She bit her lip, choking back angry words as the waiter reappeared at the table. He placed plates in front of them, offering them ground pepper and freshly shredded parmesan. He refilled their wine.

After he'd departed, Paolo took a bite of the

fettuccine, appearing coldly unaffected by their discussion.

It was all Isabelle could do not to cry.

Why had she brought up the past? Stupid. *Stupid.* Sitting up straight in her chair, she twisted a large amount of pasta onto her fork and stuffed it into her mouth.

She'd meant to imitate Paolo's calm behavior, but the butter, cheese and freshly made pasta burst onto her palate like an explosion of joy. Even when she was heartsick she could feel pleasure. It surprised her. But why should it? She despised Paolo, and feared the pain he might inflict in her life, but that didn't stop her from desperately wanting him.

"Do you like it?" he asked quietly, several minutes later.

"It's delicious," she muttered. She took another bite, then realized that she'd finished the entire plate. It was the best meal she'd had in ages. If she hadn't been in a public restaurant, she might even have licked the sauce off the sprig of rosemary garnish. "I just wish I could cook like this," she sighed under her breath.

"It could be arranged," Paolo said.

"What do you mean?"

"Armando could teach you. He is a friend of mine."

"But I'm terrible," she blurted out. "Why would you want me to try again?"

"You like to cook. You said it's one of your greatest pleasures."

She shook her head, blinking up at him in confusion. "You would spend an hour with me, in the kitchen of a trattoria, watching me learn to make fettuccine? Why? What could you possibly gain from it?"

"I told you. Your every appetite." Paolo stood up, holding out his hand. "Come. It's time for a lesson."

Paolo stared out through the tiny porthole window, watching the afternoon sun drift downward as his plane flew up the Italian coast, along the shimmering blue sea.

Damn you, I loved you. But you couldn't even be faithful to me for a single night.

The tearful expression on Isabelle's face when she'd spoken those words still haunted him. He wondered if it could be true—if she'd actually loved him. Was it possible that he'd been more to her than a boost to her vanity?

No, he told himself harshly. She'd just been slumming. She'd said so herself. If she'd actually loved him she never would have flung the ring back in his face.

But still…

He glanced down at the adjacent white leather seat. Exhausted from a long, busy day, she'd fallen asleep against his shoulder soon after their plane left Rome. Her head kept falling forward in her sleep, causing her eyelashes to flutter.

He put his arm around her. Leaning more

fully against his chest, she wrapped one arm around him with a contented sigh. Like a child clutching a beloved toy.

Why had she come back to his apartment that day?

He watched her chest rise and fall with each breath. She looked so peaceful. So beautiful. Almost as beautiful as she'd looked in Armando's kitchen. Her eyes had glowed as the chef taught her to make fresh pasta and properly melt butter in a pan. Every so often she'd glanced back at Paolo with a crease in her forehead, as if expecting him to criticize or complain. But he'd enjoyed watching her. The joy on her face as she'd patiently worked to learn a brand-new skill had made him catch his breath.

For all these years he'd known exactly who Princess Isabelle de Luceran was—a spoiled, vain little gold digger.

Now he wasn't sure what to believe.

While making the pasta, she'd gotten a large smear of flour across her cheek. He'd brought it to her attention, expecting her to panic and head for the nearest mirror. But she'd just laughed. No—she'd *giggled*. She'd tried to wipe it off with the back of her hand, only succeeding in making things worse.

Finally, he'd gently swept the flour away with his hand. She'd looked up at him, and her laughter had died away.

Holding her close, while she looked so damn sexy in that apron, Paolo had nearly forgotten that they were in the crowded kitchen of a trattoria. He'd nearly lowered his head to kiss her. Had wanted to pick her up and wrap her legs around his waist, to spread her across the clean, gleaming table…

He'd barely restrained himself. Now, he looked at her sleeping beneath his arm.

If what she'd said was true—

If she'd loved him, and she'd returned to the

apartment to give a different answer to his proposal—

Strange to think how different things might have been if he hadn't gone to his neighbor's apartment to borrow some whiskey. At the time, his choice had seemed either whiskey or a long jump into the Hudson.

His blond neighbor had answered her door wearing only a bra and shorts. "Sure," she'd replied with a grin. "I have a ton of whiskey. Here."

He'd gone back to his apartment alone, but a few glasses later she'd knocked at his door. "Can I borrow your bed? Mine's broken," she'd said brazenly.

He hadn't wanted her. Not really. But he hadn't resisted either. He just hadn't cared. What difference did it make? Sleeping with…what was her name?…Terry? Tara?…had been the same as drinking her cheap whiskey. The same buzz, the same forgetting, the same wretched hangover the next morning.

But to think if he hadn't touched her all his young dreams of marrying Isabelle might have come true…

It's better this way, he told himself harshly. Many women had tried to get him to commit over the years, but he'd always resisted. Easily. He had no intention of loving anyone. Love made a man vulnerable. The only woman he'd ever loved had left him. Even his own mother had left him as a baby. He'd be stupid to set himself up for that ever again.

Besides, he didn't need love. He had the satisfaction of a hefty bank account. The power of having others to serve him. The triumph of being the fastest motorcycle racer on earth.

Only one thing was missing. And with Isabelle that piece would finally be complete.

He would have a home.

She would bring respectability to his family

in the eyes of the world. Though at night, in his bed, she would be far from respectable…

He gently stroked her cheek. He'd seen the hurt in her eyes because she thought he'd so easily replaced her.

The truth was that Isabelle wasn't replaceable. To the contrary. She was different from any other woman he'd known. She had pride—in her family, in herself. She had dignity and self-control. It was what made her special. It was what made her valuable.

And, whatever she might think, he did value her.

She would be the perfect wife. The perfect mother of his children. She would service his needs and supervise his homes. The devotion she'd shown to her nephew proved that she was born to be a mother. And her cooking was rapidly improving…

He grinned to himself, then his smile faded.

One thing hadn't changed. On no account would he love her.

She murmured in her sleep, turning toward him with a soft, satisfied sigh. Her arm clutched him tightly, pressing her breasts against his chest.

He would possess her, body and soul.

He looked again at her full, pink lips.

He'd start with her body.

Why had he done it?

In the backseat of the limo, traveling the coast road from San Piedro airport with Paolo's arm around her, it was all Isabelle could do not to ask.

Why had Paolo allowed her to have a cooking lesson? He'd blackmailed her into becoming his mistress for one night, then given up precious hours purely to indulge her desire. He'd arranged the lesson. He'd encouraged her every step of the way.

What could he possibly gain from it? It wasn't

like she would be living with him in the future, cooking his meals.

She glanced at him from beneath her lashes.

She'd felt so close to him at the trattoria in Rome. Laughing. Touching. Mashing ingredients for the pasta, melting butter and cheese in the pan beneath Paolo's hot, approving gaze. It had all been a joy. *This must be what it's like,* she'd thought. *To be normal, to be loved, to cook for my family in a snug little kitchen...*

She thought Paolo was a cold, cruel, faithless bastard. So why had he been so kind?

"We're almost home, *bella,*" he murmured, pressing a kiss against her forehead.

It's a trick, she told herself fiercely. He wants something.

She just didn't know what it was yet.

But all afternoon he'd been like a knight out of a fairy tale, handsome and true. And she already felt like the wicked witch who'd stolen his child. If they really were in a fairy tale, some ogre would certainly have come round to eat her by now.

If only she could trust Paolo enough to tell him about his son…

"Alexander," she whispered, picturing the little boy's face. She stopped, her heart pounding with fear. If she did tell Paolo, would she hurt the child she'd always tried so desperately to protect?

Would Alexander, instead of being King of San Piedro, become just another illegitimate love-child whose parents had lied?

"Alexander?" Paolo repeated, looking down at her with amusement. "Are you worried about your nephew? It's only been a day, and Durand is safely behind bars. But if you want to go back to the palace for a quick visit…"

"No." Her teeth chattered. That was the last thing she wanted right now. She had to get through her night with Paolo.

Stretching out their time together was too

dangerous. He tempted her to betray every promise she'd made to herself. He lured her to her own destruction.

It would be too easy to love him again…

But the sun was setting. All she had to do was get through a few more hours. Just one night. Then she could go back to Magnus and, if he still wanted her, announce their engagement.

The thought of it made her sick to her stomach. She didn't want Magnus. She never had. And now, spending time with Paolo…

His large hand curled protectively over the bare skin of her arm. She looked at him in the twilight. The shape of his wide shoulders and finely sculpted chest was visible beneath the white T-shirt, and the scattering of a few dark hairs showed above his collar. His rugged jaw was dark with five o'clock shadow. He was so handsome he made her head spin.

His thigh, muscular and wide beneath the denim, pressed against hers as the Rolls-Royce twisted along the curves of the coast road. She relished the feel of him, the heaviness of his weight pressing on her; she closed her eyes, savoring his warmth and the pressure of his body. They were barely touching, but she could feel him from her scalp to her toes.

The car stopped.

"We're here," Paolo said. She opened her eyes. The villa was silhouetted in shadows against the vivid red and orange Mediterranean twilight.

Paolo got out and held out his hand. Her knees shook as she placed her small hand in his larger one, allowing him to help her from the car. But instead of leading her up the sweeping steps to the villa he pulled her toward the dark, lush gardens that overlooked the cliffs.

"Where are you taking me?" she asked.

He looked down at her, his heavy-lidded eyes full of intent. "Does it matter?"

No. Looking into his face, she felt mesmerized. Without a mind or will of her own…

He drew her through an old wooden door that led past the seven-foot stone walls guarding the secret garden. He led her past the intricately designed ponds, flowerbeds and palm trees to the nineteenth-century gazebo overlooking the cliff.

The sun was falling, plummeting like a fireball into the sea. The fading scarlet cast his sharp cheekbones and jawline with a roseate glow. She looked at his mouth. His gorgeously cruel mouth that had given her such pleasure. That had once said, *I will always love you, bella, you and only you.*

He caught her staring and she jumped in embarrassment. She'd nearly leaned forward to kiss him—another thing she'd sworn she'd never do…

What was this spell he cast on her?

She had to get a hold of herself.

"Don't worry." She straightened her shoulders, attempting a derisive laugh. "I won't be stupid enough to try to seduce you again—"

He pushed her back against the bougainvillea-covered trellis, sweeping her hair off her cheek with his large hand.

"You don't have to try, Isabelle," he said in a low voice. "You're always seducing me. Everything you say, everything you do makes me want you."

His hands cupped her jawline and the cool breeze, infused with the fragrance of roses and sea salt, blew through her hair, spinning around her and making her dizzy.

"I want you more than I've ever wanted any woman," he said, and he lowered his mouth to hers in a deep, searing kiss.

She closed her eyes, transported by the feel of his lips on hers. The unexpected tenderness of his caress made her breathless with longing, desperate with need…

"Now, at last," he whispered darkly against her cheek, "you're mine."

CHAPTER SIX

SHE'D never been kissed like this. Never. Been kissed like this.

Her body melted against him in the shadows of the garden. She could feel his heat like a raging fire. He kissed her not with the angry, bruising passion of yesterday, nor even with the naïveté of their long-ago youth, but with something in between. With the tenderness of the boy but all the fierce power of the man.

And this time his kiss had purpose. His hands grasped beneath her soft pink cardigan, his fingertips rough against her skin. He kissed her, taking firm possession of her mouth as he deftly undid her bra. She felt his hands cupping her breasts and her whole body went tight. His fingers squeezed against her nipple, causing her to gasp.

She suddenly realized that he intended to take her right here in the garden. Where—in spite of the seven-foot-high stone walls—anyone could see them. Servants. Photographers with wide-angle lenses.

"No," she breathed, struggling to resist. "Not here."

"Here," he said, holding her wrists. "Now."

Tempted beyond belief, she watched the hard, handsome angles of his face in wonder. He was like a god of nature, she thought suddenly. A savage ruler of a wild, primeval kingdom. But there were traps beneath the lush beauty—poisonous flowers and animals with sharp claws. A civilized girl could wander into his kingdom and disappear. She'd be eaten, consumed, until only the flowers feasted upon her bones.

And yet still she hungered…

"We can't…" she gasped, trying to pull away. "We mustn't…"

His knee pressed between her legs. "You can't deny me."

"Let me go," she whispered.

His fingers cupped her breasts, rubbing her nipples gently against the cashmere. "In the night," he said darkly, "in my garden, you're no prim-and-proper princess. You're a woman. *My* woman."

Slowly he lowered his head, kissing her neck, sending spasms of pleasure up and down her body. Pulling away, he looked down at her. "Do you really want to go back to the villa? To close the windows and lock the door? To hide and stifle your cries of joy?"

She didn't even have to think about it. "Yes!"

"What a sad life you lead, Princess. A sad, lonely life."

"What do you want from me?" she cried, struggling to rip her wrist out of his iron grip.

"To admit that I've missed you? To admit that I've spent ten years alone, night after night? To admit you're the only man I've ever been with?"

He grabbed her shoulders, his dark eyes searching hers. "Is it true? I'm the only man you've ever taken to your bed?"

"Go to hell!"

"Is it true?" he thundered.

"Yes!" she cried.

Anger gave her strength to pull away. Turning on her heel, she ran through the garden, away from the villa, tripping down the cliff steps to the shore. She was desperate to get away from the look in her eyes. He felt sorry for her. He *pitied* her. He'd spent a decade making love to countless women, while she'd just admitted she was a bitter, lonely spinster, pining for the one man she could never let herself have…

At the bottom of the steps was a secluded beach, an apron of white sand surrounded by rocky cliffs on three sides and the sea on the other. She turned her face toward the moonlight. The roar of the sea, the pounding surf of the rising tide, echoed the rapid beat of her heart.

"Isabelle!"

She pulled off her beige leather pumps, carrying them in her hands in the effort to run faster away from him across the sand.

He caught her.

"Don't be afraid of them, Isabelle," he said in a low voice. "Never be afraid. I'll never let anyone hurt you. If any man tried, I would grab him by the throat and toss him into the sea."

But who would protect her from Paolo?

He pulled her into his arms. She wanted him with every drop of her blood, every beat of her heart, every longing of her soul. Even if it cost her marriage to Magnus. Even if she lost everything. She couldn't fight him anymore. She couldn't fight them both. She'd lost the will to resist…

But still, as he wrapped his hands around her naked waist, she trembled.

"I'm afraid," she whispered.

"You're with me," he said.

But that's what frightens me, she wanted to say. *I'm afraid I'll give you everything...*

"This is Anatole Beach." Paolo took her shoes from her hands and let them fall one by one. "Have you heard of it?"

"Yes." She could hear the cries of the gulls overhead, echoing strangely against the large boulders of the shore and the crevices of the cliffs, as if someone was weeping. "The Russian nobleman lost his wife..."

"She drowned on their honeymoon. The next day he threw himself off that cliff."

"He couldn't bear to live without her," she whispered.

Paolo unbuttoned her cardigan, dropping it onto the sand. "Love is destructive, Isabelle. You asked why I gave it up. That's why."

I won't love you, she vowed to herself desperately. *I won't.*

He pulled off the cashmere shell over her head. Kneeling at her feet, he gently pulled her skirt down past her thighs, to her knees, finally dropping it to her feet.

Then he looked at her.

Wearing just her plain white silk bra and panties, whipped by the wind on the moon-drenched beach, she didn't feel cold. Not with Paolo here. Even surrounded by long-ago ghosts, beneath the eerie cries of the gulls, she felt warm and bright as a midsummer day as long as he was with her...

He rose to his feet.

"I loved someone once," he said softly. "Just once."

Her heart vibrated as fast as a humming-bird's wing.

Slowly, he lowered his mouth to hers. His lips were gentle. He kissed her languorously. Thoroughly. Until her knees were so weak she couldn't have stopped kissing him, even if every paparazzo on the Riviera were madly snapping pictures.

He finally released her, and she opened her eyes, exhaling. He pulled his white T-shirt off over his head, revealing bare muscled shoulders and a taut chest laced with dark hair. He pulled off his jeans, and his black boxers, form-fitting against his hard thighs, revealed how much he wanted her.

She looked into his face with stars in her eyes.

He suddenly smiled down at her. "I dare you to follow me."

Turning without warning, he raced into the surf.

She obeyed without thought, following him across the sand, running barefoot into the sea. The cold water shocked her. Then it invigorated her. She laughed with the pure joy of freedom as she ran through the waves. Dipping her hands into the water, she splashed Paolo. Water dripped in rivulets down his hard-muscled body.

With a mock roar, he turned on her. He chased her, scooping her into his arms.

The laughter faded from their faces as they looked at each other, both breathing hard.

"Isabelle…" he said hoarsely.

Somehow, she was never sure how, they made it back to shore. He lowered her to the sand, all the while crushing her lips against his own.

He touched her everywhere, caressing her in the moonlight, making her body gasp and clench and cry. The roughness of the sand pressed beneath her, threatening to devour her beneath his weight. Her lips were bruised, her body aching. She moved beneath him, straining as she felt him between her legs.

With a curse, he rolled off her, yanking down his boxers. Ripping her white silk panties off with one pull of his powerful hand, he positioned himself between her legs. For a moment he hesitated. She arched her whole body against him. If he didn't take her now…

He shuddered as she moaned his name. Drawing back, he thrust into her.

She gasped. He filled her completely, stretching her to the limit and more; he was inside her so deeply. She bucked her hips, crying out in building pleasure as he rode her. Quickly. Urgently. The roar of the rising surf grew closer as he squeezed one taut breast in his hand, biting and suckling her nipple through the wet, clinging white silk.

Holding on to her shoulder and breast, he pushed into her harder. Faster. The tension coiled low in her belly, threatening to consume her. It was too much, too fast. She tried to pull back, to slow down.

He wouldn't let her. Grabbing her wrists, he forced them above her head, holding them into the sand as he thrust deeper still, taking his full pleasure and enticing her to do the same. He wouldn't let her escape everything he was giving her...

She started to writhe and shake, twisting her head as waves of joy lifted her in pleasure so intense it was almost pain. She felt water against her feet, rushed from the lifting tide of the sea. Her body detonated like an explosion, sending shockwaves that curled her toes into the sand.

She screamed, never once caring who might hear. With a simultaneous roar, he filled her with one deep final thrust, spilling his seed into her.

For several long moments afterward he held her close.

Dazed, she licked her swollen lips, tasting the salt of the sea. She could feel the beat of his heart against her skin, and smell the fragrant breeze, redolent of spices from distant lands. She felt the waves of the surf, cooling their wet, naked bodies with each rush of the rising tide. The sea lingered like a caress, lapping against their skin.

But each time the water fell away it stole more of the sand beneath her.

Paolo woke in his bed with a start.

Something wasn't right.

Sitting up, he shook his head, hazy and disoriented. A cool breeze was blowing through the open window, waving the long, translucent curtains. Birds were singing in nearby trees. Bright sunlight cast a golden patina through his enormous bedroom, from the gleaming hardwood floor to the Savonnerie rug.

"Paolo?" From the pillow next to his, Isabelle blinked up at him sleepily. "What's wrong?"

In a rush, everything came back. Making love to her in the pounding surf. Returning to the villa, sharing a shower and making love again. Falling into bed, still naked in each other's arms. But that had been hours and hours ago. That could only mean…

"I slept," he said in amazement.

She stretched her arms over her head, blinking with a pretty, kittenish yawn. "Do I need to explain the concept of nighttime?" she teased.

"I never sleep," he muttered, suddenly sweating in the cool morning air.

Looking as if she still weren't quite awake, she held out her arms. "It's too early," she murmured. "Come back to sleep."

He turned his head to look at the gold clock over the marble fireplace mantel. "It's almost eight," he said in disbelief.

"Too early," she sighed, closing her eyes and turning against the soft pillow.

She didn't understand. How could she, without experiencing insomnia herself? She didn't know the helpless fury and rage he'd felt night after night. Paolo had always been able to fight anything and win—it was how he'd become rich, how he'd become powerful. But since the night he'd bought this villa he'd been powerless to do what all of his employees, from

Valentina Novak to his fourth under-gardener, could do without effort.

Every night he'd stared at the shadowy ceiling, waiting to hear the birds cheerfully singing his doom, waiting to face the dim horizon of dawn more exhausted than the night before. Trapped.

But somehow Isabelle had changed everything.

He cursed under his breath. It was a coincidence. It had to be. All that vigorous lovemaking last night had worn him out. There could be no other explanation.

None of the other women you've bedded helped you sleep, a small voice pointed out.

He squashed down the voice, pummeled it into dust. He wouldn't—couldn't—accept that Isabelle de Luceran had that kind of power over him.

"Paolo," she called sleepily. "Come back to bed."

"*Sì,*" he said automatically, rolling over to

take her in his arms. She closed her eyes, sighing in satisfaction. He kissed her temple, then looked down at her.

Her skin glowed the color of cream, with warm roses in her cheeks; her long chestnut hair was wild, tumbling across his pillows in a riotous cascade of shiny waves. Contentment emanated from her like a house cat curled up in sunlight. She was naked. She had no makeup, no jewelry.

She was the most beautiful woman he'd ever seen. And all he knew was that he wanted more of it. More sleep. More lovemaking. More of her.

And he would have it. Not because he needed her, he told himself, but because he enjoyed her. Making love to her. Watching her laugh. Sleeping next to her. Possessing her in every way.

Even now she might be carrying his child.

He heard her suck in her breath. Her eyes, the color of rich caramel, flew open in horror. She clutched his shoulder. "Paolo!"

"Yes, *cara mia*?" he said, idly tracing her naked breast.

"We—we didn't…" She paused, swallowing, then blurted out, "We didn't use a condom!"

"Is that all?"

"Is that *all*?" she cried out. "Don't you realize what could happen?"

"Be calm," he said sharply, softening his tone with a smile. "You have nothing to worry about."

She blinked up at him, looking as if she wanted to believe him so badly that she could barely breathe. "I don't?"

"No," he said firmly. "You will not end up pregnant and forced to raise a child alone. That is quite impossible."

"Oh," she said. Then, more quietly, "Oh." She turned to him, and her eyes were enormous. They were pools of light, teasing him with goodness and trust.

Yes, he thought, mesmerized by that light.

"Do you mean that you—?"

"Come here," he said, pulling her naked body to his.

He took her in his arms and made love to her again, this time more slowly. He caressed her satin skin, spread her wide, filling her. Slowly. Inch by inch. Until she begged for more. He held himself back, making her moan and writhe before bringing her to fulfillment—twice.

Only then did he let himself go, closing his eyes, pushing into her with a hard gasp. He didn't enjoy her for nearly as long as he'd planned, however. He'd intended to make her climax a third time, but she turned the tease back on him, grabbing his hips, stroking between his legs and up his body with feather-light touches. *Dio santo*, he was only a man.

Afterward, as he rose from the bed, he was glad he'd decided to make her his bride. A lifetime of such nights with her wouldn't be enough to satiate him.

Smiling to himself, he ordered breakfast on

the intercom. As they waited for its arrival he dressed, pulling on a long-sleeved black shirt and fine-cut Italian pants. He could feel her watching him from the bed, where she was still tucked beneath his quilt, lazing with contentment like a Sunday morning.

Marrying her would be a honeymoon that never ended.

Oh, yes, he thought, congratulating himself on his choice. Mrs. Caretti. He liked the sound of it. His wife. In his bed. At his command.

His British butler brought in a tray of breakfast delicacies and placed it on the small round table near the fireplace. Smoothly he set plates and served the food before departing, never once showing any indication that he recognized Princess Isabelle de Luceran in his employer's bed.

But at the door the butler turned and said with a cough, "Sir?"

Frowning, Paolo went to him. "Riggins?"

"You asked for the newspapers, sir, as always. But… ah…I thought I might give them to you privately. For the sake of the lady."

As Riggins departed, closing the door behind him, Paolo looked down at the open papers in his hand.

And immediately closed them. He ground his teeth. Damn the paparazzi to hell. He cursed the photographers and their long-range lenses, and most of all he cursed his own arrogant certainty that they'd have privacy on his own damned beach…

"Don't look!" Isabelle cried.

"What?"

Without thinking, he looked. Isabelle had leapt naked out of bed and run across the bedroom. She was standing on her tiptoes, stretching her lovely limbs to reach for his robe, hanging on the bathroom door. For a moment his eyes traced over her, helpless to do anything but savor the curving lines of her exquisite body. Only after she'd wrapped the tie twice around her waist, covering herself with white cotton terry from her neck to her ankle, did his brain start to work again.

She sat back down at the table, glancing at him with a flush of self-consciousness on her cheeks. "You didn't see anything, did you?"

He tucked the newspapers behind his back. "Nothing I didn't want to see."

Her blush deepened. "You're a beast, Paolo. A beast."

"*Sì,* I know." He gave her a wicked grin. "Although you didn't seem to mind that last night."

She smiled at him for a moment, glowing. "No, I didn't."

Her face grew serious.

"Our night is over," she said softly. "Our time is done."

No.

It was a visceral response from deep inside

his soul, fierce and possessive. He put his hand over hers.

"I don't want our affair to end, Isabelle," he said in a low voice. "We are both free. Stay with me."

She looked down miserably at her plate, loaded with Spanish *jamón*, fried eggs, and two big, buttery slices of *tarte aux fraises*.

"You are free, Paolo," she said. "I am not."

His brows lowered like a stormcloud. "What do you mean?"

"I told you two days ago."

"You cannot still intend to marry him!"

"Magnus can give my country a future."

"Do you love him, then?" he demanded. "Are you really such a fool?"

"I'm Princess of San Piedro. My fate is to serve my people." She looked up at him, her light hazel eyes limpid and pure. "I have no choice but to accept it."

"You'd be sacrificing yourself for no good cause." Furious, Paolo tossed the newspapers across the table in all their lurid glory. "Perfect as he is, do you think he'll still want you when he sees this?"

She blanched as she read the headlines. Snatching up the first tabloid, she opened the pages to see pictures of them making love on the beach, fuzzy, but still distinct enough to reveal their faces. Gasping, she grabbed the next paper, which had a similar picture on the top right corner of the front page.

"You said we were safe!" she cried.

"I thought we were," he said grimly. "My mistake."

Her beautiful features crumpled. Tossing down the paper, she put her face in her hands, rubbing her forehead. "I've ruined everything. I never should have… Oh, my God. It looks like a deliberate insult!"

He clenched his jaw. "I'm sorry."

She bit her lip. "It's all right," she said in a small voice. "It wasn't your fault."

But it *was* his fault, and he felt it. He'd seduced her on the beach, promising her he would protect her. That he hadn't kept his promise felt like a knife-wound in his chest.

"I'll find that photographer and smash his camera," he added, barely joking.

She laughed, hiccoughing through her tears. "Yes, please. That would be lovely." Then she shook her head, furrowing her brow in anguish. "Magnus will have seen these pictures. My *mother* will have seen them!"

In a controlled motion, he poured himself a *tazza* of espresso. "I'll talk to them. Tell them it was my fault. Settle them down." *Tell them you're mine,* he added silently.

She stared at him. "Are you out of your mind? You can't do that!"

"Why not?"

"Well, you're not exactly my mother's favorite person, for a start. I doubt Magnus would even agree to meet you."

"He would," Paolo said tersely.

She shook her head in disbelief. "Because you always beat him in every motorcycle race? Just because you're rivals doesn't mean—"

"No. That's not why." He gulped down some espresso, barely feeling the burn against his tongue. "Magnus isn't just my rival, Isabelle. He's also my brother."

"Your *brother*?" she gasped.

But it suddenly all made sense. For the first time Isabelle saw the similarities between the two men. The same hard jaw, the same cleft in the chin. Magnus was more slender, more elegant. Paolo was darker, rougher, wider. But no wonder she'd once thought Magnus to be handsome—his coloring, the beauty of his dark eyes, had reminded her of Paolo.

"Brothers," she breathed. She shook her head. "How is that possible?"

"We had the same mother."

"Magnus's mother...the Princess von Trondhem? She was a society matron from an old New York family!"

"Yes, I know." He finished his espresso off in a gulp. "When she was sixteen she eloped with my father. By the time I was born she knew she'd made a huge mistake. My father was hard and dangerous, which she thought romantic. Until she lived with him." He gave her a thin smile. "She wanted to leave, but he wouldn't let her. So right after I was born they made a deal. He gave her a divorce. She gave him—me."

"Oh, Paolo," she whispered, her heart breaking for him.

He shrugged. "It apparently wasn't difficult for her to leave. Her family sent her to Europe to wait for the scandal to blow over, and she met a prince in Vienna. Within weeks she was married. A year later she had a new son." He stood up. "From the day my brother was born everything was given to him on a silver platter."

With a jaw like granite, he turned away.

"Paolo…" she whispered.

"I have some work to do," he said over his shoulder. "Finish your breakfast, and then we will talk." He stopped, looking back at her. "You're going to stay, Isabelle. We both know it. Don't waste your time fighting me."

He closed the door firmly behind him.

She stared after him, aghast. His mother had *left* him. As a baby. How did anyone ever get over that?

She suddenly had a horrible headache. Her own parents hadn't exactly created a warm home. Between her father's endless affairs and her mother's bitterness, their rare family dinners had been filled with many cold silences. But at least she'd had her brother, and later Karin. And at least Isabelle had always known that both her parents had wanted her.

She still remembered how horrible it had been to return to San Piedro ten years ago, pregnant, unwed, and apparently forgotten by her faithless lover. Her mother had spent the whole flight home alternating between sympathy and plotting to give away the baby. Isabelle had alternated between weeping and throwing up. Until Karin had come to her with a compromise.

"No one outside the family need ever know." Her sister-in-law's eyes had filled with tears. "Your brother needs an heir, and if I have another miscarriage I'll die of grief. Help us. Let us love your child as our own."

It had nearly killed her to give up Alexander, but she'd done it. For her family. For her country. And most of all—for Alexander.

But even though he'd never called her *Maman*, Isabelle had at least spent every day with the boy. She'd experienced his childhood, planned birthday parties, laughed at his knock-knock jokes and soothed his tears over skinned knees. She'd been the boy's confidante, his friend.

Paolo didn't even know he had a son.

She'd stolen his son away without even giving him the choice to be a father.

He obviously doesn't want children of his own, she argued fiercely. He'd told her yesterday that she would never end up pregnant and alone. It had taken her a few minutes to figure out what he meant, but of course a man like Paolo—working sixteen-hour days, spending his free time motorcycle-racing and romancing one glamorous mistress after another—wouldn't want to be slowed down by the responsibilities of a family.

He'd had a vasectomy.

But not wanting children and dealing with them if they came were two different things.

When he'd spoken about his mother she'd seen a vulnerability in his eyes that she'd never seen before. His jaw had been tense and angry, his shoulders tight, his body poised for a fight. But she'd still seen the truth: he'd never gotten over being abandoned as a newborn. It still angered him. Bewildered him.

It forced her to finally admit another truth to herself.

She was falling in love with Paolo all over again.

She was falling desperately, totally in love with a man she could never marry. Whom she'd hurt in the most cruel way possible.

"Oh, my God," she whispered from bloodless lips. How would he feel if he found out that she'd forced him to unknowingly abandon a child— just as his mother had once abandoned him?

She couldn't love Paolo. She couldn't. The secret she carried would always be between them. What she'd done was unforgivable. If he ever found out he would hate her for all the days of his life.

And yet…he deserved to know. Even if it did make him hate her, he had to know he had a child.

If she told him, could she trust him to keep

the secret? Could she trust him to protect Alexander above all else?

Suddenly she couldn't breathe. Then she rose to her feet. She squared her shoulders, tying Paolo's robe more firmly around her. Trying not to think about what she meant to do, she walked down the hallway and down the stairs.

She turned in the first door on the right and saw walls of books—the library. A man rose from the upholstered chair by the window.

"Oh!" she said surprised. "Excuse me, I—"

She started to turn away, then froze. As if in slow motion, she looked back at him.

Prince Magnus von Trondhem stood silhouetted in front of the wide, expansive windows in an elegant gray suit and purple silk tie.

"Hello, Isabelle," he said quietly.

His expression was calm, almost kind, but her cheeks went hot with shame. She was wearing Paolo's robe. Her hair was mussed with lovemaking. And since he was here he'd obviously already seen the pictures of her making love to his brother.

"Magnus," she whispered, barely able to speak over the lump in her throat. "I'm so sorry. I never meant to hurt you…"

"It's all right. He's the one to blame, not you." He held out his hand. "I came to tell you that you're making a mistake. And to offer a warning—get out before it's too late."

CHAPTER SEVEN

Paolo stared blankly at his laptop screen.

With a sigh, he looked up at the wide window above his desk. It was a beautiful spring morning. Sunlight glittered against the sapphire water, and the fragrant breeze made the sail-boats and yachts in the harbor dance and sway.

He'd just made love to the woman of his dreams three times. He had no doubt that his plans would be successful. Whether she realized it or not, she would soon be his bride.

So why wasn't he happy?

Closing his laptop in disgust, he rose from his desk and paced the length of his study. Going out onto the open balcony, Paolo stared at the blue water and the gently rocking boats. He raked a hand through his hair.

He never should have brought up his mother. Some secrets remained better buried. What difference did it make that she'd left? What difference did it make that she'd loved his perfect brother and not him? He didn't care. Being left alone had only made him stronger. He'd learned to fight. He'd learned to win.

"Sir?"

Turning around, he saw Riggins, red-faced behind him on the balcony. The usually dignified butler was breathing hard, as if he'd run across the length of the villa.

"*Sì?*"

"We've been looking for you," Riggins panted, then leaned forward, trying to catch his breath. "Prince Magnus von Trondhem—here. He's—waiting in—the library."

"Magnus is in my library?" Paolo demanded. "You just let him in?"

Riggins looked shocked. "Mr. Caretti, you said if the Prince ever should visit, you'd wish to see—"

"That was before." Paolo cut him off. Scowling, he strode back through his study without a backward glance.

Halfway down the hall, he heard a man's voice. He froze at the base of the wide, sweeping staircase. His hand clenched against the banister, every nerve taut as he listened to his half brother's muffled voice coming from the library.

"He'll never marry you, Isabelle. Never be faithful to you. He's dangerous—ruthless. He's not from our world. He doesn't have our code of honor. The way he wins on the Grand Prix circuit year after year—it's suspicious. And I wouldn't be surprised if the whole time he's been seducing you he's still been sleeping with that secretary of his…"

With a muttered growl, Paolo knocked the door aside with a loud bang. He took in the scene at once: Magnus, suave and elegant, with his hand on her shoulder; Isabelle, still wrapped in his oversized robe, clutching the belt in her white-knuckled hands and looking stricken. Looking small. Fragile.

Paolo went straight for his brother.

"You had something to say to me?" he demanded.

"Just the truth," Magnus replied coldly. "If you really care about Isabelle you'll let her go, before you cause any more damage to her reputation."

Paolo's lip curled.

"I'm not giving her up. Not to you or anyone."

"That's for her to decide, isn't it?"

They both looked at her.

Isabelle's hazel eyes locked with Paolo's for a long minute before she finally turned to Magnus.

"It's all right," she said faintly. "Really. You can go, Magnus. I'll be fine."

He pressed his hand against hers. "When you change your mind, come to me," he said urgently.

"I still want to marry you, Isabelle. Our union can be successful. When you finally realize what kind of man he really is, come to me—"

"Time to go," Paolo growled. Brother or no brother, he wasn't going to stand and watch the man try and convince her to leave him. He grabbed Magnus's shoulder and started walking, shoving him down the hall.

"But—"

"Thanks for the visit." Pushing him out the front door none too gently, he closed the door behind him and turned to find Isabelle standing behind him.

"Is it true?" she whispered. "About the… the cheating?"

He clenched his fists. He should have punched his brother in the face for even daring to make that accusation. Damn his sense of family obligation anyway. He ground his jaw. "Since he can't beat me, he accuses me of cheating. He's a liar—and a loser. I work. I train. I never stop. So I win."

She took a long, deep breath. High above them in the foyer, the enormous crystal chandelier cast prisms of light and color across her lovely drawn face.

"That's not what I meant," she said. "What he said about your secretary. I met her in New York, remember? She's…beautiful."

"Yes, she is," he said tersely. "It doesn't mean I'm sleeping with her."

"I wouldn't blame you if you were. It's not like we're married." She swallowed, her troubled eyes translucent as amber. "It's not like you love me."

He met her gaze evenly. Honestly.

"No, I don't love you, Isabelle. And I never will."

His words should have given her a sense of relief. The last thing she wanted was for him to love her. Bad enough that she was already starting to fall for *him*.

If he loved her in return, she would never have the strength to pull away. Even knowing that staying with him would ultimately destroy her.

"Good," she said numbly. "I'm glad to hear that. Now, if you'll excuse me, I…I need some air…"

Turning on her bare heel, she all but ran out onto the balcony. Once she was alone, she turned her face toward the sea. She pulled the plush robe closer to her body, shivering in the fresh morning breeze. She could hear the cool wind through the palm trees, waving the green fronds above her in the bright blue sky.

She'd nearly made the biggest mistake of her life. If she'd told Paolo that he was Alexander's father their lives would have been tied together forever.

Would Paolo have demanded marriage? Would he have forced her to be his bride? Would he have used his charm and strength and body to make her love him forever, even against her will?

If he had, how long would it have been before he betrayed her? Immediately? By announcing to the world that he was Alexander's true father? Or ten years from now, by taking a young mistress when Isabelle started to lose the first blush of youth?

Magnus was right—there was no telling what Paolo might do. He wasn't of their world. He didn't have the same code of honor.

She'd be reckless to take the risk. Certifiably insane.

She had to marry Magnus as soon as possible. Because it terrified her that, in spite of everything, she was desperately trying to think of excuses to stay…

She heard Paolo come up behind her.

"I'm sorry if those weren't the words you wanted to hear," he said quietly. "I told you I'd never lie to you."

"You're wrong." She whirled to face him. "I'm glad you don't love me. It would only complicate things."

"Love is a waste of time," he agreed.

"Right," she managed over the lump in her throat. "And anyway, I'm leaving today."

"No, you're not." He came closer to her.

She lifted her chin. "You can't stop me, Paolo."

He stroked her cheek. Slowly he lowered his mouth to hers. His kiss was passionate. Tempting. His lips were hard, soft, sweet. His tongue stroked between her lips, teasing her, spreading her, and he drew a shuddering breath.

"You're mine, Isabelle," he whispered against her skin. "Magnus doesn't deserve you. You're a bright flame, a tropical bird of paradise. He isn't man enough to hold you."

"And you are?" she breathed.

"Yes," he said in a low voice. "I will hold you forever."

She wrenched her head away so he wouldn't

see the confusion and desire and pain tumbling inside her. "I have to marry. I want a family, Paolo, someone of my own. Can't you understand that?"

He looked down at her. "That's why you're going to marry me."

"What?" she gasped.

His eyes were dark, mesmerizing. "I have factories of my own. Influence of my own. Together we will be an unstoppable force. You will marry me."

She sucked in her breath. For a moment she was tempted. No man had ever affected her like Paolo. He could give her a life of excitement and joy, of racing motorcycles along the sea and making love all night long. Each morning would be better than the last. Every day would be bright and new with the man she loved beside her.

So he'd cheated on her, she thought suddenly. So what? He'd done it once, and he would likely do it again. Her mother had dealt with it. Couldn't she? Wasn't a lifetime of being Paolo's wife worth occasionally turning a blind eye to his infidelities? She could endure that private humiliation, couldn't she, if no one else ever knew?

She took a deep breath.

No.

She'd seen her mother's anguish too closely. Jealousy and bitterness poisoned a woman. Loving Paolo, and knowing he took pleasure in other women, would kill her.

If infidelity was inevitable, she wasn't going to make the mistake of marrying a man she loved. It was better to marry a man who left her cold. That was the safe choice. The only choice...

"Our marriage will be better without love," he said softly, stroking her cheek.

Better for you, she thought. Better so he could sleep with his gorgeous redheaded secretary and whomever else took his fancy with a clear conscience.

Heart in her throat, she turned her head away. "I can't."

"Can't?" he growled. "Or won't?"

"It's the same thing." She clenched her fists together, trying to stay strong. "When I marry, I must choose someone who can lead San Piedro."

"Someone royal," he said evenly. "Not someone like me."

Suddenly she felt like weeping. "Don't you realize what it would mean for you to marry me?"

"*Sì*," he said. "But I still want to."

"You'd make an awful prince!" she cried. "You'd never handle the public criticism. You'd go ballistic at the lack of privacy. And as for diplomacy—" She tried to smile. "You'd get mad and tell some head of state to go to hell."

"You still don't trust me," he said evenly. "You never have."

He'd told her the truth about not loving her. She had no choice but to return the favor.

"No, I don't," she said softly. "I can't. I'm sorry."

Muttering a curse under his breath, Paolo turned away. And watching him go, she felt a bolt of anguish crack her soul apart, like lightning scorching the dry earth.

Everything she'd said was true. It all made perfect sense.

But her instincts were screaming. Her whole body cried out for him. And her heart...

Paolo, I love you.

As if of its own accord, her hand flew out to grab his wrist. "Wait."

"For what?" he asked in a low voice, not looking at her. "You've made your opinion of me plain."

"Please." For a moment she couldn't breathe. "Just wait."

She felt herself standing on the edge of a precipice. She heard the voices of Magnus, of her mother and brother and Karin, and the ministers of San Piedro, all telling her to return to the palace at once. To be dignified. To be proper. To be good.

To follow the rules.

But it's the twenty-first century! she cried back to them. Dignity and sacrifice weren't what they used to be. A neighboring crown prince had lived openly with a commoner— a single unwed mother—before he'd made her his bride. Another crown prince had married a woman from a family so scandalous that her parents had been excluded from the wedding.

Why should Isabelle sacrifice every bit of personal happiness for old-fashioned standards that the rest of the world had long since left behind?

I can't give him up, she thought suddenly. *I won't. Not yet!*

She needed a taste of pleasure. A drink of joy. That was all she wanted. She was starving for it—gasping like a fish on sand. A few weeks of passion and excitement and laughter with the man she loved would fill her soul enough to sustain her for the lifetime of duty.

A vacation. That was what she needed. From being a princess. From being herself.

And then I'll go back, she promised herself desperately. *I'll marry Magnus. I'll be good and follow the rules the rest of my life.*

Perhaps it might even help. After a few weeks with Paolo she would surely see his faults and fall out of love. Or else he would grow tired of her and betray her. At any rate, she could then marry Magnus for the good of the country, knowing that she had left nothing behind—except, perhaps, her own heart.

And a heart, she thought, was something she was quite willing to live without…

Taking a deep breath, she came to her decision.

"I can't be your wife, but…"

"But?"

"I'll be your mistress," she whispered.

"My mistress?" Paolo's dark eyes were assessing her, luring her, scorching her whole body. "You would openly live with me? You would defy the whole world?"

"Yes." Looking up into his handsome hard-edged face, she said the words she'd longed to say her whole life. "Paolo, teach me how to live dangerously."

Isabelle wasn't the only one who soon found herself living dangerously.

Over the next few weeks, in spite of Paolo's warning instincts, he found himself starting to do something he'd sworn he would never let himself do again.

He found himself starting to like her.

Respect her.

And more…

He'd enjoyed teaching her to ride a motorcycle. She'd followed his instructions to the letter, screaming with joy as she took her first solo ride. With paparazzi following close behind, they'd had to drive fast.

He'd taken her to Paris for dinner—but with bodyguards and flashing photographers following them everywhere they went, they'd practically had to sit atop the *Tour Eiffel* to watch the sunset over the violet rooftops.

Finally, on her birthday, he'd been so fed up with the constant media assault that he'd kidnapped Isabelle on his yacht and taken her out onto the open sea. They'd had a candlelit dinner alone on deck, and he'd presented her with sapphires from Bulgari, emeralds from Van Cleef & Arpels. With fireworks exploding in the dark sky above his yacht, they'd made love until dawn. It had been perfect.

Until pictures taken from a long-range helicopter had appeared in a British tabloid the next day. So much for the open sea!

Damn it, how was a man supposed to seduce

a woman into accepting his proposal if they could never be alone?

She would accept his proposal soon enough, he told himself. In his arms by day, in his bed by night, she would soon realize she could not challenge his will. She had no choice but to become his bride.

In the meantime, there was no reason to slow down on his plan to get her pregnant…

They spent a great deal of time in bed. A good thing, because they couldn't leave the villa without an entourage. Paolo almost felt like a prisoner in his own house.

Still, she was worth it.

Isabelle, on the other hand, took the paparazzi in her stride. He admired her for that. She never complained. No matter the inconvenience or pain, she waved for the crowds, her smile always in place.

Paolo didn't take it nearly so well. She'd been right about one thing—the constant lack of privacy set his teeth on edge. But he'd wanted the most famous princess in the world, hadn't he? It was all part of the deal.

Still. He should have tossed that photographer into the sea when he had the chance, he thought with a growl. Then at least there would be one less of them.

He'd thought the frantic interest couldn't last. Their relationship was just scandalous and new. The hard-edged Italian-American tycoon stealing a virginal princess from another man on the eve of her reported engagement made great copy. Paolo told himself the interest would fade.

And yet the media furor only intensified. Two weeks ago a German tabloid had discovered that Prince Magnus von Trondhem was his secret half brother, and the news had landed like a bombshell all over the world. Since then reporters had camped along the road outside his villa, desperate for pictures, shouting questions at the closed windows of their limo when they left the gate:

"Princess Isabelle, why did you choose one brother over the other?"

"Yeah, was one better in bed?"

"Was it love at first sight?"

"Do you have any intention to marry?"

That last question was one that Paolo himself longed to answer—preferably while throttling the obnoxious reporter who'd asked it. *Yes,* he wanted to yell at them. *We're going to marry. Leave her the hell alone.*

But throughout it all Isabelle was calmness and grace personified. One hot day she even ordered lemonade and teacakes be taken to the reporters camped outside the villa's gate.

"Why?" Paolo had demanded incredulously. "Let them leave. Or die of thirst," he'd muttered, only half-joking.

She'd just given him a rather wistful smile. "Do you really want them to write stories about us in that mood? We can't control what they write about us. But we can try to influence their opinion."

Sure enough, the stories posted the next day were all about Isabelle the Kind, Isabelle the Bountiful, who still remembered poor reporters while living in sin with a rapacious Italian-American billionaire.

"See?" she'd said, flashing him a smile.

And he did see. Dealing with reporters and media was as much of a negotiation as sculpting a business deal. Only instead of trying to purchase a company, he was trying to gain percentage points in public approval.

Something he'd need to work on after they were married. But Isabelle had been doing it since birth. From now on, he decided, when it came to reporters he would follow her lead.

She managed reporters so well, he could hardly wait to see how well she'd raise their children…

Every day now he watched her. Wondering if

she was pregnant. For weeks their lovemaking had been hot and furious. Each time he'd waited for her to ask for a condom, to ask why he wasn't worried about pregnancy. He'd already told her his intention. He would have gladly told her again.

But she didn't ask.

Which could mean only one thing. Part of her must want to marry him, in spite of all her stated objections.

Oh, yes. Their marriage would happen. Within weeks, if not sooner.

As he became wrapped up in their affair, playing hard and making love and sleeping in her arms each night, he respected her more and more. And he realized he didn't want Isabelle to just supervise his houses and rear his children.

He wanted her to be the heart of his home.

Home... He savored the thought. As a boy, he'd longed for a real home, the kind where people looked out for each other and celebrated holidays together. Family dinners. Teaching his son to play catch. Teaching his daughter to write her name. But to have a home he needed the right woman.

Now he had her.

Isabelle might not love him, but love came through in everything she did. She was all heart—and he realized that, foreign as it was to him, he needed that in his life.

Isabelle would be the heart of their family.

He would be the gate, keeping them safe, keeping them all from harm.

Isabelle was his now. No matter what she might believe, Paolo wouldn't let her marry any other man on earth. She belonged to him, and no other woman would do. No other woman had her grace, her fire. Her strength.

In Isabelle he'd finally found a worthy partner. A woman who challenged him both in and out of bed. A woman he could respect.

Finally he'd found a woman he could trust.

CHAPTER EIGHT

"WHERE have you been?"

Paolo's voice was teasing, almost tender, as he came up behind Isabelle in the foyer of the villa. He wrapped his arms around the waist of her demure white sundress of eyelet lace. "You've been gone for hours."

She whirled around in his arms, hiding the brown paper bag behind her back. "I was busy at the palace," she said, unable to look him in the eye. "I had breakfast with Alexander, then a meeting with the French ambassador."

Pulling back, he frowned at her. "I called the palace. They said you left an hour ago."

"Oh. Yes." She gave a feeble attempt at a

laugh. "I forgot. After I finished speaking with Monsieur Fournier, I went out with Milly."

Alexander's nanny, only a few years older than Isabelle, was the one who'd gone to the drugstore to buy the test. She was the only one she could count on not to sell the story.

Isabelle's chic goddess sandals tapped nervously against the mosaic floor.

"Rough day at the palace?" His voice was sympathetic as he rubbed her shoulders with his strong hands. "Your mother keeps you busy."

"Avoiding her keeps me busy." She gave him a weak smile. "You've been busy too, training for the race and planning Caretti Motors' expansion."

"Valentina is bringing me construction bids right now," he said. "She should arrive in about an hour."

"Oh. Valentina. Good." Just what she needed—to be faced with Paolo's devastatingly gorgeous redheaded secretary at the very moment when she herself wanted to stick her head down the toilet. "Valentina is a charming person," she managed. "So stylish and... smart."

She despised the way her voice trembled. Would he notice? Would he demand to know what she was hiding behind her back? The telltale evidence was in her hand right now, barely covered by brown paper.

"So you don't mind if I work until the race starts?"

She gave him a faltering smile. "I have to spend the afternoon at the palace anyway. It's my mother's birthday. She'll disinherit me if I don't go for a visit."

"Ah. Guess it's time to bite the bullet." He gave her a cocky grin. "Think there's anything in particular she wants to discuss with you?"

With a gulp, she looked down at the floor. "Perhaps."

She was trying not to think about the conversation that awaited her—the lecture she'd managed to avoid for weeks. But at the moment even that seemed easy to endure compared to her newest fear…

"I'll miss you." His smile became sultry and predatory as he looked down at her. He looked handsome in a black T-shirt and dark jeans, tanned and fit from their hours spent sunbathing together on his yacht and driving along the coast. "It'll take at least an hour for me to properly bid you farewell."

She swallowed. Normally, spending an hour in bed with Paolo was the most exquisite enjoyment she could imagine, but she just couldn't do it. Not now. Not when her whole future was hanging by a thin line.

It's not possible, she told herself for the hundredth time. It can't be. Once I take the test I'll see I was ridiculous to even worry about it.

She couldn't be pregnant.

She was Princess of San Piedro, second in

line to the throne. She couldn't have allowed herself to get pregnant again. By the same man.

Without love.

Without marriage.

She wasn't eighteen anymore. She was constantly followed by press. If she were pregnant, this time she wouldn't be able to hide it. She would be scorned and mocked around the world. Just taking Paolo as her lover had already created shock around the world, causing damage to her image. To her country. And, she feared, to Alexander.

Alexander—her cheeks flamed just picturing how the scandal would affect him if she were pregnant by her Italian-American lover. How it would affect her innocent babe.

There's no baby! She shouted at herself. Paolo's had a vasectomy! But her hands shook, crumpling the top of the paper bag as she turned away from him.

"I'm…just not in the mood," she said, and it

wasn't even a lie. "I'd better go. I'll see you at the Grand Prix."

She'd never turned Paolo down for sex before. Not once. She could feel his surprise as he watched her.

"As you wish," he said after a pause. His voice sounded awkward, stilted. "I need to test-drive the engine adjustments anyway. I'll give you a ride to the palace."

"That's not necessary," she said, still not meeting his gaze. "I'll see you at the race."

He grabbed her wrist as she turned to leave. "What's wrong, Isabelle?"

"Nothing." *Just that you have a secret child and might soon have another...*

"Really?" His tone was decidedly cooler in turn.

She had to get out of here. Once she took the test she would tell him her fears, and they'd both have a good laugh. Once she knew she wasn't pregnant everything would be all right again, and she could cheer him on to victory in the race.

She'd promised herself that she would end their romance after the Grand Prix, but now that it was here she couldn't do it. She wanted to put it off. Just a few more days. A few more weeks.

Nine more months?

Her breath caught in her throat.

If she were pregnant, it meant that Paolo had either casually risked pregnancy, not caring how it might affect her, or that he'd deliberately done it to cause her pain.

He wouldn't do that, she told herself angrily. He wouldn't ruin my life and an innocent child's life. I believed the worst about him once. I'm not going to do it again.

I love him…

"Bella?"

She ripped her arm from his grasp. She couldn't take the test here. She couldn't even look at Paolo's face until she knew for sure. "I have to go."

"Fine. I'll tell Yves and Serge that you want to leave."

She could feel hurt mixed with anger radiating in waves from him. But she didn't stop to wait for her bodyguards. She needed to be alone. Going to the garage, she climbed into her custom pink MINI COOPER convertible, put on her sunglasses and wrapped her hair in a scarf. As she drove past the paparazzi camped outside the villa, she was glad her face was hidden behind the big black lenses.

She didn't want anyone to see the fear in her eyes.

I'm not pregnant, she repeated to herself numbly. *I can't be.*

But she was late.

She drove faster along the coast road, evading a persistent photographer on a Vespa behind her. For a moment driving made her forget her fears as she focused on the skills Paolo had taught her.

Accelerate, brake, turn.

Accelerate, brake, turn.

But once she was behind the gate of the *palais*, safely past the cobblestoned courtyard with her car tucked into the royal stables, she picked up her carryall and stared at the crumpled brown paper inside with mounting fear. Then she slammed the car door behind her and started toward her private apartments in the palace.

She found her way blocked by Chancelier Florent, her mother's advisor.

"Thank you for coming, Your Serene Highness," he said sternly in French, in the tone that had used to terrify her in childhood. "The Queen Regent is anxious to discuss your marriage prospects."

She rubbed her forehead. "Yes, I know. I'll…be there in just a moment."

"It's Her Majesty's birthday. Perhaps you've forgotten?"

"No, I haven't forgotten. I just have something to do in my own apartments first…"

"I will follow you then, *mademoiselle*." His voice dripped disapproval. "And wait until I can escort you into the Queen Regent's presence."

Take the pregnancy test with dour-faced Florent waiting outside her bathroom door? She knew when she was beaten. "Very well." Tucking her handbag safely under her arm, she pulled the scarf off her head with a resigned sigh. "I will see her now."

Queen Clothilde's harsh lecture in the *salon de réception* soon made Isabelle long to return to Florent's friendly warmth.

"I cannot believe that any daughter of mine would be such a *fool*." The slender gray-haired woman paced back and forth across the dais. "He cheated on you once already. He nearly destroyed you. Was once not enough?"

"He's not going to hurt me, *Maman*." But even as she defended Paolo, Isabelle didn't know whether she could believe her own words. Was she pregnant? After all his talk about honesty, could he have lied about his vasectomy?

"That you would even *dream* of letting that man back into our lives…"

"He saved Alexander. Does that mean nothing to you?"

The Queen stopped. "Of course it means something," she snapped. "I am grateful beyond words that he saved my grandson from that kidnapper. But it would have been more appropriate to reward him with a note and a gift—not your virtue!"

Isabelle met her mother's steely gaze. "You know he took that long ago."

The Queen Regent clenched her jaw. "And while you flaunt your affair, our country is suffering. We need you to marry a man who can make difference."

"I love Paolo, *Maman*," she said quietly.

Her mother drew in a ragged breath, then sank wearily into the throne.

"He is a heartless playboy, *ma fille*. He will string you along and…"

"He's asked me to marry him," Isabelle said.

Clothilde looked at her in amazement. "And what was your answer?"

"It was no," she whispered.

"Thank the good stars for that." Her mother shook her head. "You cannot marry Paolo Caretti. You realized that long ago. It's why you gave away your child. Do you think to reverse your decision now, and make an alliance with his family? He has no manners. No morals. He's nothing. A *nouveau riche* motorcycle racer, barely fit to be a chauffeur. The son of a common thug—"

"But Paolo's not like his father!" she cried. "He's different. He can be trusted. I think. I hope…"

"Is that so?" The Queen Regent pressed her advantage. "Have you trusted him enough to tell him the truth about Alexander?"

Isabelle swallowed, fell silent.

Her mother waved a hand. "You've grown old before your time. I see now that you need time to enjoy yourself before settling down. So I forgive you. Your *paramour* is racing in the Motorcycle Grand Prix this afternoon, *oui*? His participation brings desirable attention to San Piedro. So wait until after the race. But tomorrow," she said sharply, "you will end it. You will go to Prince Magnus and beg him to take you back."

"But I don't love Magnus!"

"Consider that the best wedding gift you'll ever receive," her mother said coldly. Florent came into the room, and she waved Isabelle's dismissal. "Go. I have no desire to watch you weep into my birthday cake all afternoon. Go and enjoy one last night with your mechanic. But tomorrow I expect you to do your duty."

Isabelle left the *salon de réception* feeling despondent and cold. It was exactly what she'd known her mother would say. And she couldn't even argue.

But Isabelle wanted to trust Paolo. She'd already given him her heart. After weeks of spending her days and nights with him she hadn't found a single flaw.

Except for the fact that he would never love her…

"Aunt Isabelle!"

She stopped when she heard the childish whisper. Turning, she saw Alexander peeking around a suit of armor down the hall. She held out her arms and the little boy threw himself into her embrace. She held him close for a moment, relishing the feel of his thin arms around her, the smell of his shampoo. After enduring her mother's tirade, Isabelle wanted to hold her son in her arms forever. But when he pulled back she reluctantly let him go.

Blinking back tears, she looked down at him in wonder. "How is it possible? I swear you've grown since breakfast!"

"I know," he said, straightening with dignity. "An inch in the last month. Milly has been letting me eat all the ice cream I want. Hard just keeping meat on my bones, she says."

"I'm glad," she replied with a smile. She couldn't stop looking at him. Her son. Her baby. At nine years old, he was still a child, but quickly growing into a man. And looking more like his father every day.

Alexander frowned. "Is *Grandmère* angry with you?"

"Yes."

"Why?"

She rubbed the boy's back with a sigh. "She wants me to marry someone. But now," she said wistfully, "I realize I want to marry someone else."

"You mean Paolo Caretti?"

She drew back in shock. "How do you know about him?"

"Of course I know him. I'm not a baby, Aunt Isabelle. He saved me in the farmhouse from that bad man. I like Signor Caretti. He's nice. And in the garden you seemed to like him too." He tilted his head. "Why doesn't *Grandmère* like him?"

She cleared her throat. "It's a long story."

Alexander squared his shoulders. "Well, if you want Signor Caretti, I will give you my permission. As your King," he said grandly. "Not just my permission—my *blessing*."

For a moment Isabelle just stared at him. Her son was giving her permission to marry.

Images of the last weeks of joy came rushing at her. She could marry Paolo? She could have that—for a lifetime?

Her whole idea of existence suddenly crashed down around her. Perhaps he didn't love her, but her love might be enough for both of them. He cared for her. Could that be enough? As long as she could trust him not to hurt her…as long as she could trust him to protect Alexander…

Mon dieu, she thought. The pregnancy test would prove he'd never lied to her. It would come back negative and prove she could trust him.

In a rush of emotion, she kissed the top of the boy's head.

"Thank you," she whispered.

But when she reached the elegant marble bathroom of her private apartments all thoughts of trusting Paolo flew from her mind. She took the test and realized her future didn't hang just on one thin line, but two.

She was pregnant.

Pregnant.

She whispered the word soundlessly, her hands trembling as she drove her MINI COOPER out of the palace gates. She'd wanted to trust Paolo. She'd almost convinced herself that she could.

And he'd lied to her.

Or had he? She searched her mind. He'd never *said* he'd had a vasectomy. He'd only said that she'd never find herself pregnant and alone.

That suddenly had a whole different meaning.

I'm planning to seduce you, get you pregnant with my child, and make you my bride.

He hadn't lied to her. He'd flat-out told her the truth from the beginning.

Her fingers clenched on the steering wheel as she drove down the steep cobblestoned street. Sunlight was everywhere, the warmth of the Riviera smiling on the southern Mediterranean port, but she felt ice-cold.

She saw a Vespa pull out from a corner to follow her. The paparazzi were relentless, as always.

She sucked in her breath.

What would the papers say when they found out she was pregnant?

What would her mother say?

And Alexander… Would he hear the whispered insults? Would he be forced to defend his aunt's apparently easy virtue?

She was suddenly desperate to feel Paolo's arms around her. She drove more quickly along the road, trying to outrun the Vespa behind her. Paolo would make this all better. He would solve everything. Somehow he would convince her to forgive him.

After all, he hadn't lied to her. He'd told her the truth. She just hadn't believed him.

Nothing had changed. She could still marry him. *Why shouldn't I?* She thought defiantly. She loved him. She was pregnant with his child.

She could perhaps endure a marriage with love only on her side—if only she could trust him not to betray her. As long as he was faithful, she thought she could love enough for both of them…

Paolo's not a liar, she whispered through chattering teeth as she arrived at San Cerini. *I can trust him.*

She parked near the stone fountain in the circular driveway. Her eyes fell upon the large statue of the phoenix rising from the waves, clutching a sea dragon in its sharp claws. The bird's beady stone eye seemed fixed on her as she walked toward the steps. As if it were trying to tell her something.

I can be that phoenix. I can rise above my fear, she told herself. *I can forget the past. I love Paolo. I can tell him everything. I can even tell him about Alexander. He will forgive me. I can trust him...*

Stepping from the sunlight into the shaded cool of the foyer, she felt a rush of strength and hope. She was pregnant, but it wasn't a disaster after all—it was her chance to do everything right. Just because every man she'd ever known had been faithless it was no reason to be afraid. Paolo was different. He was honorable and true and—

Where was he?

She stopped in the doorway of his empty

study. He'd said he would be working with Valentina on the factory bids. He'd been so busy with Isabelle lately his work had started to suffer. He was probably trying to get through as much of it as possible so he could focus on the motorcycle race later. And then he'd be free for hours of laughter and making love...

"Paolo?" she called.

"I think he's upstairs, *signorina*," a passing maid told her shyly.

"*Grazie.*" She ran up the stairs toward their bedroom. Perhaps he was taking a nap; she'd certainly done her best to wear him out last night. If he was asleep, she would take off her clothes, climb in under the covers and thoroughly wake him. She grinned to herself happily. Then she would tell him her news, the way she'd dreamed of sharing similar news ten years ago...

"Don't worry," she heard him say. "She won't be back until tomorrow."

Isabelle stopped abruptly outside the bedroom door.

"Are you sure?" It was Valentina's voice, a sultry Czech purr.

"Of course I'm sure," he said impatiently. "Isabelle will never know. And even if she did, she likes to share. So come here. Yeah, there. This is what you want. I'm tired of hearing you beg. Do you want me to wait outside while you take off your clothes?"

"No," the woman sighed. "I trust you…"

Frost spread up and down Isabelle's body. She could barely feel her fingers or toes as she gently pushed the bedroom door aside.

The redheaded secretary was standing near the closet. Her blouse had been tossed carelessly to the floor. She was wearing only a skirt, high heels, and a sexy bra that pushed her enormous breasts halfway up to her neck.

Paolo was sitting by the window, his laptop on his knees. No doubt waiting for Valentina to come round and entertain him with a sexy strip-tease while she moaned out figures from the quarterly reports.

Isabelle's whole body felt like ice. Especially her heart.

Slowly, she turned to face Paolo.

"Isabelle." He rose to his feet. "You're home early." He cleared his throat with what he no doubt hoped was a charming grin. "I hope you don't mind, but I wanted Valentina—"

"Oh, but I do mind," she said hoarsely, swaying on her feet. Blood was rushing through her ears like a torrent of rain. She looked from the father of her children to his half-naked secretary. "How could you?" she whispered. "How could you do this to me?"

The expression on Paolo's face changed.

"No," he said sharply. "*No.* Wait."

But she couldn't wait. With a sob, she turned on her heel. She ran down the stairs and out the front door.

As she started the engine of her car, the large stone phoenix grinned down at her. Only now she realized her mistake.

She wasn't the phoenix.

She was the dragon in its claws.

"Isabelle!" she heard Paolo shout behind her. In her rearview mirror, she saw him running down the steps toward her. But she didn't wait. She gunned the motor and drove right out of the gate. She didn't slow down until she reached the von Trondhem villa half a mile away.

She would do her duty. She would marry Magnus.

She never, ever wanted to see Paolo again…

A whimper escaped her lips. She stopped her car, staring at the von Trondhem crest on the wrought-iron gate.

She couldn't do it.

No matter how Paolo had treated her. She loved him. She couldn't marry anyone else. She couldn't betray Paolo the way he'd betrayed her.

She pounded on her steering wheel in frustration, then with a sob she leaned her head against the dashboard and cried.

CHAPTER NINE

"Where's the Princess, *signore*?"

Paolo looked up from a motorcycle engine, a wrench still in his hand. His racing bike had already been taken to San Piedro by his team. For the last hour he'd been taking out his aggression on the 1962 Triumph Bonneville he'd been patiently restoring over the last year. Motor oil coated his fingers, slick like blood.

"I don't know where Isabelle is," he muttered, lowering himself back under the engine. "And I don't care."

He'd thought he'd been doing a kindness for Valentina by letting her try on Isabelle's dress. His secretary had gushed about it for an hour, and he'd been frankly sick of hearing her talk about the photos of Isabelle at Cannes. It was just a dress, for God's sake. Isabelle wouldn't care if she tried it on. She rarely wore the same thing twice anyway. Clothes were just a uniform for her—like his old mechanic's jumpsuit or his current Savile Row suits.

But of course Isabelle had taken one look at them in their bedroom and believed the worst. Paolo had been facing the window, going through the numbers on his computer; he hadn't even *wanted* to turn around and look. Valentina Novak was a good secretary, but she wasn't his type—and even if she had been he never would have dishonored Isabelle that way. Not in a million years.

But when had Isabelle ever trusted him? Never. He'd never been anything but honest with her, but no matter what he did she refused to believe he was decent or true.

So fine. If she wanted to pout and run away,

fine. He would be damned if he would explain a single thing to her.

Bertolli made a worried sound with his tongue. "I only ask about the *Principessa*'s whereabouts because I have just heard René Durand has escaped custody of the San Piedran police."

Paolo rolled out from under the engine. "What?"

"The police wanted to ask him about some recent art thefts, and he escaped during the transfer. It's probably nothing," Bertolli said hastily. "I'm sure he's halfway to Malta by now, on some fishing boat. Don't worry about it, *signore*. We should head for the race. It's almost time…"

Paolo's breathing suddenly came hard. "Does the palace know about Durand?"

Bertolli reluctantly nodded. "They're the ones who called me."

"Everyone is safe?"

"Yes." Bertolli paused. "But the *Principessa*'s

convertible isn't here. Yves and Serge are trying to find her. You know that Durand had that grudge against her…"

"*Maledizione,*" Paolo swore. Throwing down his wrench with a loud clatter, he leapt to his feet and headed for his fastest street-legal motorcycle. "Offer the police our assistance with Durand," he bit out. "If they don't want it, send some men out anyway. I want to know where he is. I want him found."

"*Sì, signore.*"

As Paolo roared his motorcycle past his gate, he ground his teeth. *Damn her!* Why did she have to be so stubborn? Why couldn't she just trust him?

But beneath the anger his heart was pounding with a totally different question.

Why hadn't he gone after her?

Isabelle. Just thinking of her in Durand's clutches made him feel sick.

He loudly accelerated past the waiting paparazzi, who scattered like dead leaves in the wind. Once he hit the coastal road, he let out the throttle.

He passed her pink MINI convertible headed the other way. He had a brief vision of Isabelle: dark sunglasses, tight red lips, shiny chestnut hair blowing in the wind.

Then she was gone.

He turned his motorcycle so hard that he left a black scar against the pavement. Gravel scattered as he braced one leg against the ground in a tight hairpin turn. He caught up with her at San Cerini.

Not bothering to go past his driveway, Paolo brought his motorcycle to a screeching halt. He knocked over the kickstand and stalked angrily through one of the open garage doors to where she was parking her car. Bertolli was gone and his mechanics had already left, so the garage was strangely empty.

Isabelle looked pale as she climbed out of

her convertible. Her hand seemed to tremble against the gleaming pink paint. Looking at him, she slowly took off her sunglasses.

He wanted to yell at her. To demand that she never, ever go anywhere without him ever again. He wanted to knock sense into her.

Instead, he took one look at her miserable face and his whole body went rigid. Before she could say a word, he took her in his arms.

For a moment she tried to push him away. Then she sagged against him. He heard her choked sob, muffled against his chest.

"I didn't sleep with Valentina," he vowed, stroking her hair. "I've never touched her."

"I want to believe you," she whispered. "I want to."

"So believe me." He looked down at her. "You're the only woman for me, Isabelle."

Pulling away, she gave him a tremulous smile that didn't fool him for a second. She rubbed her nose, and her eyes were red. "I'm fine, really."

"Why are you crying?"

"It's hay fever."

"Like hell it is." He knew her now. Knew the way she trembled, and the shape of her, and the way she cried out joyfully at night when he thrust into her. And he knew to his marrow that she was hiding something. "Tell me what's wrong."

She pushed back from him so violently that she stumbled and nearly dropped to the concrete floor.

He caught her. She weighed almost nothing at all. He had to convince her to eat more, he thought dimly. For the last few days she'd had no appetite, barely touching her food. He'd thought it wasn't his responsibility to make sure that she ate. Now he realized that it was. Everything concerning Isabelle's health and happiness was his responsibility.

"What is it?" he said quietly. "Tell me."

Covering her face with her hands, she fell against him with a sob. Shocked, he held her in his arms, rocking her gently against his chest like a child. Sunlight beamed through the garage's solitary window, shimmering on motes of dust floating softly through the air. At this moment even time seemed suspended.

And he realized how much he cared about her.

Enough to protect her from anyone—anything.

Even if she didn't trust him, he trusted her. She was the one person who would never lie to him.

The one woman he might even let himself… love?

"Did someone hurt you?" he asked in a low voice. "Was it Durand?"

If Durand had hurt her, Paolo would rip the man apart with his bare hands…

She drew back with a confused frown. "Durand? No. Why?"

"It's nothing," he said quickly. There would be plenty of time to share the news of the man's escape when her eyes weren't full of tears. As it was, seeing her cry was driving him so crazy he could barely think straight. He wanted to comfort her. He had to make her tears stop. "So where did you go?"

She licked her dry lips. "I went to see Magnus."

"Magnus?" His heart stopped in his chest. "Why?"

"To accept his proposal of marriage," she said quietly.

He stared at her for several seconds. His brain couldn't understand her words. It kept re-ordering them, but they didn't make sense.

He dimly looked at the tools spread across the garage, the wrenches and engines and pneumatic lifts. At the old Triumph Bonneville parked between his gleaming red Ferrari and brand-new white Lamborghini. They hadn't changed since the afternoon. They were still solidly the same.

So how was it possible that in that same space of time the rest of his world had been ripped apart without warning?

He wanted to hold Isabelle tight, to never let her go, to demand that she stay.

But he knew it was no use.

She'd made up her mind that he couldn't be trusted. And it was finally clear that nothing he did would ever change her opinion.

Abruptly, he let her go.

"Leave, then," he said. "I won't stop you."

Turning away, he started to walk out of the garage.

With a cry, she ran to him, blocking him from the door, throwing herself into his arms. "I couldn't do it! I couldn't even drive past his gate. I don't want Magnus. I never did. I want you, Paolo. *You!*"

His heart, which had been flash-frozen in his chest, abruptly started beating again. He could again feel his limbs, feel the blood rushing joyfully back through his body.

She didn't want to leave.

She trusted him enough to stay.

He sucked in his breath, looking down at her searchingly. "So you believe me, then? About Valentina?"

Biting her lip, she looked away. Her shoulders straightened as she seemed to come to a decision, and she looked him full in the face.

At last she was going to say she believed in him. That he was a man of his word. That he was nothing like his father.

That she trusted him the same way he trusted her.

The future was wide open before them. It wasn't too late. Perhaps they'd never be the same innocents they'd been during that long-ago summer in New York, but that was all right. Because now they both knew how rare it was, how precious a gift it truly was, to find someone who made you want to risk everything…

"You deserve to know." She closed her eyes and took a deep breath. When she looked at him, her caramel-colored eyes swirled with emotion. "Whatever happens, you deserve to know," she repeated softly to herself. "You deserve to know."

"What is it?"

"I can't keep it secret anymore. I don't have the right. No matter what kind of husband you would be, you have the right to know about this."

"What?" he demanded, growing alarmed by her wide eyes, her pale expression. She looked as if she might faint. Instinctively, he braced her body with his own.

"Alexander isn't my nephew. He's my son." Taking his hands in hers, she clenched them to her chest and looked up at him fiercely. "Paolo—Alexander is your son."

"Son?"

She watched the blood drain from his face.

"Yes," she whispered. "It's true. Paolo, we have a child—"

His hands dropped hers. He staggered

backward as if the concrete floor had just lurched beneath his feet.

She reached for him, trying to grab his hands, desperate to steady him. "I wanted to tell you. I tried to tell you!"

"No." His eyes were wild. He pulled away, not letting her touch him, leaving her hands grasping only air. "He can't be my son. He is nine years old. You wouldn't have…you couldn't have lied to me all this time."

"Please, Paolo. You have to listen!"

He turned to her, and his eyes burned like a raging fire. "Your brother needed an heir to his throne, so you gave him our baby?"

"That's not how it happened!"

"You gave away my son!" he said, as if he didn't hear. "You took him from me. You tossed our baby away as if he meant nothing to you at all. What kind of heartless mother could do that?"

"Do you think I enjoyed it?" she cried. "Giving

him away nearly killed me! Having him call me Aunt while he called someone else *Maman*…"

His eyes darkened, and she realized that she'd only reminded him that at least she'd seen their child grow up—he had not.

She took a deep breath, gathering her emotional strength. She had to stay rational and reasonable. It was the only way to make him understand. "I didn't know I was pregnant when I ended our affair. But we were young, and everything was against us. I was afraid to marry you. The differences in our social class. I knew you'd be mocked and scorned. You don't know what it is to be royal. You would have had to give up all your personal freedom…"

"And so instead you gave away our child?" he demanded.

"When I realized I was pregnant—" her voice quivered "—I tried to come back to you. I convinced my mother to give you a chance. I practically danced the whole way to your apartment…and then I saw…I saw you kissing that woman."

"That's your excuse for lying to me for ten years?" he said incredulously. "Because I sought comfort in a one-night stand?"

"I thought I couldn't trust you!" she cried.

"Right. Because I'm dangerous. The son of a criminal. You felt you had to protect our son…from *me*." He folded his arms, staring down at her with narrowed eyes. "And all this time you've been my lover, lying next to me in bed, you've never changed that opinion."

"I was afraid! Telling you meant risking Alexander's Kingship, his custody, his life! Did you expect me to ignore all that?"

"You stole my son!"

"I'm sorry!" she said, tears in her eyes. "I tried to tell you. But the more time I spent with you, the more I started to…care. I was afraid that if I told you the truth you would hate me!"

"You were right to be afraid." She could hear

the hoarse rasp of his breath. "Because I will never forgive what you've done, Isabelle. *Never.* You abandoned our child. And by not telling me you forced me to abandon him too. You've lied to me for nearly ten years. Every day for the last month you've been in my arms. And still you kept your silence. Every night, sleeping next to me, you lied. Every smile, every kiss was a lie."

"I made a mistake," she whispered. When he still wouldn't look at her, she took her heart in her hands and slowly fell to one knee in front of him. The concrete floor felt cold against her skin. But not nearly so cold as the current of fear coursing through her body. Her teeth chattered and she barely contained a sob as she, Princess of San Piedro, did the unthinkable.

She knelt before him.

Clutching his hands in her own, she pressed them against a cheek wet with tears. "Please forgive me, Paolo. Please," she whispered. "You have to forgive me."

For a moment he was silent. She could feel him staring down at her. He pulled one hand down to touch her head, reaching to stroke her hair, as if to comfort her. Even now, after everything she'd done, his first instinct was to comfort her when she cried.

She held her breath, praying, aching to feel his touch…

But at the last second, a centimeter from touching her, his hand froze. "You still don't believe me about Valentina, do you? You still think I slept with her."

She looked up his body to meet his eyes pleadingly. "Just tell me the truth. I think I could forgive you if you would just respect me enough to tell me the truth."

"The truth?" He looked at her scornfully. "Why should I bother? You've already made up your mind."

"What else do you expect me to believe? I saw you in the bedroom—"

"I expected you to trust me," he said. "Believe in me. That's what I expected. But I see now that I was expecting the impossible." Grabbing her wrists, he yanked her to her feet. He quickly released her, as if touching her contaminated him.

"My God," he whispered, raking his hand through his dark hair. "I have a son. A son who thinks I abandoned him."

"Paolo—"

"Does the boy know?" he demanded.

"No. And I don't want him to. He adored his parents. He is still mourning them."

His dark eyes looked at her incredulously. "And you don't think he should know he has parents who are still alive? *Dio santo*, you want him to go through life believing he's an orphan?"

"The alternative would be to tell him that I gave him away before he was born, and that the parents he loved lied to him his whole life. Do you think that's better?"

Clenching his jaw, he looked away as if he couldn't even bear to look at her. "The truth is always better."

"You've never told me a lie?" she said quietly. "Not once?"

He ground his teeth. "No, Isabelle. Not once."

"You never had a vasectomy, did you?"

He stared at her. "What kind of question is that?"

"You didn't use a condom," she said bitterly. "And I never asked. I thought you were joking when you said you intended to get me pregnant."

"No," he lashed out. "I told you the truth from the beginning. I wanted you to be my wife. I wanted to get you pregnant." He gave a harsh laugh. "But it's a good thing I failed, isn't it? You'd likely have given our baby away to the first person you met."

It was like a slap in the face. "That's a horrible thing to say."

"You deserve it." His eyes were dark with hate as he looked at her. "Just the fact that I have one child with you is almost more than I can bear. Thank God we don't have more."

She could hardly breathe from the pain and hurt. How could she tell him that he had succeeded in getting her pregnant?

"You're so beautiful, Isabelle," he said. "But that's a lie, too. You're not beautiful. You're ugly through and through."

"Paolo, please—" Her voice choked on a sob. "I never meant—"

"*Basta.*" He turned away. "I have to go. The motorcycle race is about to begin."

"No!" she said tearfully. "Forget the race, Paolo. Stay and talk with me."

He took his leather racing coat from the hook on the wall. "I'm not giving it up. Not for you or anyone." He gave her a hard, bright smile.

"Racing is what I do. It's who I am. I don't have a wife to slow me down, so I'm the fastest in the world. I'm alone. So I win."

"Please." She clutched his sleeve, following him out of the garage. "You can't leave me like this."

"Oh, no? Why not?"

"Because I love you," she whispered.

For a split second his eyes widened. Then his expression grew hard, his eyes even darker and more full of angry shadows than before. "In that case there's one thing you can do for me."

"Anything," she said, her heart in her throat.

"You can pack all your belongings and get the hell out of my house." Climbing onto his motorcycle, he put the key in the ignition. "Expect a call from my lawyer about custody of Alexander."

And, gunning the motor, he left Isabelle choked by dust and tears in his driveway.

CHAPTER TEN

SHE'D gambled everything—and lost.

No. Isabelle put her hands over the flat belly of her white lace sundress. She hadn't gambled everything. She hadn't told him she was pregnant. He hadn't let her.

Just the fact that I have one child with you is more than I can bear. You're ugly through and through.

She covered her face with her hands as a sob rose to her lips. He didn't want another child with her. Fine. He would never know this child was his. She would run away, disappear, and he would never know…

But she couldn't do that. Alexander. Oh, my

God. To hurt her, Paolo was going to try to get custody. He would destroy their son's life…

"Princess?"

A woman's voice, deep and breathless, spoke from behind her on the driveway. Not bothering to smooth the tangles of her hair or wipe away the tears streaming down her cheeks, Isabelle turned.

Valentina Novak stood in front of her, swaying nervously from one high-heeled foot to the other.

"What do you want?" Isabelle said hoarsely.

"I…I wanted to say I'm sorry. I just wanted to try on your dress. It was silly. I never should have…" She gave an embarrassed laugh as her cheeks turned bright red. "I never came close to fitting into it anyway. But you just have this perfect life. I thought if I tried on the dress I might feel…"

"Perfect life?" Isabelle gave a harsh laugh. "Which part of it do you envy? The paparazzi who stalk me to the bathroom? The counselors who arrange every aspect of my life? Or a palace that's cold even in summer, with thread-bare antiques I'm not allowed to touch?"

"I meant Paolo," Valentina said quietly. "I would give anything to have a man love me the way he loves you."

Isabelle sucked in her breath. "Paolo doesn't love me."

"Anyone with eyes can see that he does."

"He doesn't, and he never will. He's said it to my face."

"Perhaps he's said that with words." Valentina tilted her head, blinking at her. "What has he said with his actions?"

A torrent of images went through Isabelle. Paolo's laughter, the way he held her at night. The way he insisted she follow her passions, whether it was making fettuccine or riding a motorcycle. The way he'd taught her to accept pleasure, to face her fears. The way he'd protected her. Believed in her. Respected her.

I will always protect you, Isabelle. I protect what's mine.

I'll always tell you the truth, even if it hurts.

Her knees suddenly felt weak. She nearly sank to the ground.

This whole time she'd been so afraid that he would betray her. But *he* wasn't the faithless one. *He* wasn't the criminal.

She was.

He'd loved her. And she'd betrayed him. Not just once, but many times.

Every time she'd kept silent about Alexander.

Every time she'd believed the worst of him.

Every time she'd run away from him rather than stay and fight for the truth….

He loved her.

She slowly lifted her chin. The warrior queens of her ancient line rose up in her blood. Power and strength flooded through her as she set her jaw.

She'd been a coward. But no more.

This time she would stay and fight. This

time she would try to prove that she was worthy of him.

"Bless you, Valentina," she said, briefly grasping her hand. "Thank you."

She raced back to the garage. Climbing into her pink convertible, she dialed Magnus's number. When he didn't answer, she left him a message. "I'm sorry, Magnus, but I must decline your offer after all. I've realized I'm completely in love with your brother. I'll be there cheering for him today."

She dialed Paolo's number, but he didn't answer either. Of course not—he was either lining up for the race or ignoring her. No matter. She put the key in the engine. She would go to the race. She would tell him the truth about her pregnancy at once. There would be no more secrets between them, ever.

She would make Paolo forgive her. If he scorned her apology today she would keep trying. Forever, if that was what it took.

She would prove that she was worthy of his trust.

And he would forgive her. He had to. He was her love. Her family. The father of her children.

He was her home.

She turned the key again, but the engine stubbornly refused to start. She tried again, then pounded the dashboard in frustration. She'd coasted back from Magnus's gate on gasoline fumes, but she'd been so upset at the time that she'd barely noticed. Now, with the race starting soon, the cliff roads would already be a tangle of snarled traffic and closed streets…

She looked past the Lamborghini and the Ferrari to Paolo's sleek chrome Caretti motorcycle by the garage door, the key still dangling from the ignition.

"Oh, no," Valentina said, following her gaze. "Surely you're not thinking…?"

"It's the only way I'll make it in time,"

Isabelle said, hoisting up the white skirt of her sundress and throwing one leg over the motorcycle. "He gave me lessons. I know what to do."

"Just a few lessons, and you're going to drive along the edge of those cliffs?" The redhead shuddered. "Aren't you afraid?"

Isabelle blinked, then shook her head. "Only of losing Paolo," she realized aloud.

As she drove out of the gate she was surprised to see that the paparazzi were gone. No doubt they were camped by the finish line of the race, hoping to get a photo of the Princess and the motorcycle champion together. Blessing her unusual anonymity, she drove down the cliff road as quickly as she dared, weaving around the steadily increasing traffic.

She turned to take a short-cut on a gravel path that led beneath the cliffs—a secret way to the palace that only the royal family and their bodyguards knew about. She smiled to herself, knowing she'd arrive in plenty of time.

Perhaps she could even kiss Paolo for good luck before the race…

But as she went past a thicket of trees, a scattering of long, sharp nails punctured her front tire. The tire blew out, causing the motorcycle to suddenly wobble and veer wildly to the left. She threw her hands up to protect her face as the cruiser careened straight into a thick pine tree. She had the experience of flying, falling. Pain searing her head and arms. When she woke a minute later she was lying in grass, and she blinked in confusion up at the sky.

A man's head suddenly looked down at her, blocking the sun. He was dark and dirty, as if he'd been hiding in the forest for days, and his face was half hidden in shadow. But she recognized him at once. He'd haunted her dreams ever since he'd kidnapped her son.

"Hello, Your Highness," René Durand said. He gave her a chilling smile. "I've been hoping to catch you."

* * *

"I hope you're happy."

Paolo was pacing inside his tent, strangely unsettled. He'd gone through the final checks on his engine. His bike was already at the line. But something didn't feel right. He was tapping his helmet against his leather-clad hip when he looked up and saw Magnus standing in the doorway.

"I'm ecstatic," Paolo growled back. "It's another chance to beat you."

His half brother folded his arms. "I meant about Isabelle."

Paolo was still reeling at the news that Alexander was his son. He had a child—a nine-year-old boy he'd *abandoned* thanks to her.

"I don't want to discuss her." Paolo could hardly believe she'd claimed to love him. *Love*, he thought bitterly. Grinding his jaw, he changed the subject. "Oh, and by the way, if you ever accuse me of cheating again, I'll smash your face."

Magnus looked at him in alarm, then sighed. "You can be ruthless, you know. In the business world. On the racing circuit. You're just so much more successful than everyone else. You can't blame me for wondering if—"

"I win honestly," Paolo bit out.

Magnus put his hand on his hip. His own racing suit was angelic white and blue—a stark contrast to Paolo's devilish black and red leather. "I'm starting to believe that."

"Terrific," Paolo said. "Now, do you mind getting the hell out so I can get ready for the race?"

"Where is she?" Magnus looked from side to side, as if he expected Paolo might have hidden Isabelle somewhere behind all the gear. "I just want to tell her there's no hard feelings."

"Packing to leave, I expect." Paolo's closet had become full of her clothes over the last month. Pretty dresses, matronly blouses, seductive lingerie. Tonight when he went home they would all be gone. He would return to an empty closet and an empty house.

Good, he told himself angrily. Love him? She didn't even respect him. She'd proved that more times than he could count.

But Magnus was shaking his head. "No, old chap. She's here. She left me a disgustingly cheerful message that she'd be cheering you on to victory." He sighed again. "Like you really need the help, *hein*?"

All Paolo's uneasiness came rushing back. "When did she leave that message?"

"An hour ago."

Even in traffic that should have been enough time. More than enough.

He stuck his head through the tent flap. "Bertolli?"

The man came to him at once. *"Sì, signore?"*

"Have you seen Princess Isabelle?"

Bertolli shook his head mournfully. "No, but

Signor Caretti, the race is about to start. You need to go to the line."

"That's my cue," Magnus said. He gave Paolo an elegant salute. "Good luck to you. I'll see you at the finish."

"Wait," Paolo said sharply. He turned back to Bertolli. "Have the police found Durand?"

"They're trying, but he hasn't shown up on any plane, ship or train list. He's just disappeared. Shall I send more of our men to assist?"

A sick, hollow feeling filled Paolo's gut.

Durand.

And Isabelle.

Both missing…

"You need to go to the line, *signore*," Bertolli said. "You're going to be disqualified—"

"So I'll be disqualified!" Paolo shouted back. "It's just a race!"

Shaking his head, muttering under his breath in Italian, Bertolli disappeared.

But Magnus didn't move. He stood watching Paolo, his eyebrows raised.

"Just a race?" he asked quietly.

Clawing back his hair, Paolo took a deep breath. If anything had happened to Isabelle he'd never forgive himself. He'd promised to protect her. *Sworn* to protect her. And he'd failed. He hadn't protected her from the photographer on Anatole Beach. He hadn't made sure her bodyguards were with her when she left the villa. He hadn't warned her that Durand had escaped.

He'd just tried to get her pregnant without her consent.

Maybe she'd been right not to trust him. She'd betrayed him by not telling her about their child—yes. But he'd made a few mistakes of his own...

A sudden memory flickered through his mind. Her accusing eyes, her sad voice: *You never had a vasectomy, did you?*

He hadn't paid attention at the time, but now the obvious reason for such a question made him gasp. He hadn't failed. She *was* pregnant. Isabelle, their son, another child…all hanging in the balance because he'd been too stupidly proud to admit the truth.

"You *love* her," Magnus said. "I thought you were just playing, but you really do love her. Enough to lose what you value most."

"Yes," Paolo said wearily. And that was exactly why he hadn't wanted to love her. Love meant loss. He'd been determined to be alone forever. Hell, he'd become the fastest motorcycle racer in the world so no one would ever catch him. But he hadn't been fast enough. In spite of his best efforts he'd fallen in love with her. He knew that now.

Because he'd never felt loss like this.

Going back into the tent, he grabbed his cell phone off a table. "I think René Durand might have her."

"Durand? The art thief?"

"He's more than just an art thief—" But before Paolo could open his phone to call the police, it rang in his hand. He looked at down at the phone. An unidentified number.

"Hello?" he demanded.

"I have something you value."

Paolo recognized the sly voice. "If you hurt her, I'll kill you. Not even the vultures will find your bones."

"Write this number down. Are you ready?"

Holding the phone against his ear, he grabbed a pen from the table and looked for paper. He motioned sharply to Magnus, who ambled over with a bemused expression.

"*Sì*," Paolo said tersely. "Go ahead."

Durand gave him a long number, which Paolo wrote on his brother's white leather sleeve.

"As soon as I get the money in my account," the ex-bodyguard said, "I will tell you where to find her." The line went dead.

"What's happened?" Magnus asked.

Paolo snapped the cell phone shut. "She's been kidnapped."

"Kidnapped?"

"Contact the police." He tossed him the phone. "See if they can trace the line."

"But…where are you going?"

Paolo thought of the seagulls he'd heard, the strange echo of Durand's voice. "I have an idea where they could be."

"I'll come with you."

"No. I could be wrong. Brother, I need you to help me. To take charge. Get the police, the palace bodyguards—everyone you can find." He went out of the tent. "Bertolli! Get our men. Follow Prince Magnus's orders until I return. But first—transfer this amount to this account."

Magnus was talking on the phone, so Paolo just pointed at the numbers on his sleeve. Bertolli's jaw dropped. *"Sì, signore,"* he said faintly.

Grabbing his motorcycle from the nearby start line, Paolo pushed it through the crowds.

"The police will be here in minutes," Magnus called. "You should just wait."

Paolo threw his leg over his sportbike. "I can't."

"They're already on their way."

Forget the race, Paolo, she'd begged. *Stay and talk with me.* And he'd turned his back on her. Threatened her. Abandoned her.

Would he be too late to save the woman he loved? Too late to save their unborn child?

Paolo started the engine. *I love you, Isabelle,* he told her silently. *Just hang on. I'm on my way.*

"What do you expect to accomplish alone?" Magnus demanded.

Paolo's fingers tightened around the throttle.

"I expect to get there faster," he said, and with a loud roar of his engine he accelerated his motorcycle past the crowds in the race he'd trained for all his life.

* * *

"Good news," Durand called to Isabelle from the lowest ledge of the cliff above her. "Your lover has decided to pay. He really must care for you. If someone demanded a hundred million euros for *my* mistress, I would tell him to take her and good riddance."

Isabelle tried to raise her chin and tell him to go to hell, but there wasn't enough fight left in her. After the accident, Durand had used a stolen car to take her to this beach. He'd tied her bruised, aching body to a rock overlooking the place where she and Paolo had famously made love. It amused his sense of irony, he'd said.

"So you'll let me go?" she said through cracked lips. He had to let her go. She had to survive for the sake of her child…

"Maybe. If the money arrives in my Swiss bank account before the tide." He shrugged. "But probably not. Easier just to let you stay where you are. No witnesses."

She wanted to plead for her unborn child, but

she knew that telling him she was pregnant wouldn't make him merciful.

If she'd only been stronger, more able to fight him off. If only she'd heeded Paolo's repeated insistence that she always travel with bodyguards…

Blindly, she stared past Durand, past the rocky cliffs above. "Paolo will kill you for this. He will—"

But her last word ended on a gurgle as a wave crashed against the boulder where Durand had bound her against the rising tide of the sea.

"Don't worry, I wouldn't dream of separating you," he replied absently, plugging numbers into his cell phone. "As soon as I have my money I'll send him to join you."

At his words, Isabelle struggled against the cords that bound her wrists and ankles, but she'd spent the last hour being taunted by Durand and battered by the tide. The water was already up to her shoulders, and every wave splashed higher.

She had to stay calm and think. She had to save Paolo and the little life she was carrying inside her. She had to think of a way. Something. Anything.

Still staring down at his cell phone, Durand gave a sudden howl of triumph. "It's there. The money's there. He's paid it!" He snapped it shut with a laugh, then looked at her. "I'm afraid that means I have no more use for you, *ma chérie.* I'll bet you're wishing now you'd let me take that Monet, aren't you?"

Another powerful wave crashed into her, sending water into her mouth and nose and lungs. Salt water flooded her eyes, it drenched her ears, and she couldn't see or hear. She coughed and gagged, gasping for breath as the wave receded.

But then, as she opened her eyes, she saw a miracle in watery colors as blurred as an Impressionist painting.

Paolo came out behind Durand from the dark shade of the trees. With a roar of fury he knocked the ex-bodyguard into the dirt. His cell phone skittered off the cliff, slipping noiselessly into the sea.

With a curse, the ex-bodyguard fumbled in his pocket, drawing a pistol that gleamed black in the sun. "You're too late, you tricky Italian bastard. The money is mine—"

Paolo knocked the pistol aside. The two men fought, rolling back and forth on the edge of the cliffs above her. René Durand, with his broad shoulders and hard muscle, was a tough fighter, and wasn't afraid to fight dirty. But Paolo didn't seem to feel the man's punches or kicks. He was grim. Relentless.

"You should have just come after me." Paolo pushed him against the ground, bashing his head against the hard-packed earth. He punched Durand so hard that Isabelle could hear the impact against the bone. "You bastard—why couldn't you just come after me?"

"Paolo!" Isabelle screamed, and another wave crashed against her, longer this time. She couldn't see. Couldn't breathe. She couldn't escape her ropes. "I'm down here! Hurry!" The wave slowly receded, but only to her chin. "Save our baby," she said softly.

She took two long, deep breaths as another wave slowly built…

"Isabelle!" Paolo shouted. Tossing Durand aside like a ragdoll, he sprinted down the cliff path toward her, nearly skidding off the edge in his desperation to reach her.

Their eyes met, and she knew he wouldn't make it in time.

She was going to die. She and her unborn babe with her.

"I love you," she whispered, knowing he wouldn't be able to hear her over the waves and the pounding of his running feet.

The wave hit her, water caressing her face all the way up to her forehead. She held her breath as long as she could, but to no avail. She felt Paolo splashing around her, beneath the sea, desperately trying to free her from the cords that bound her to the boulder. She felt his frustration, his terror. She wanted to tell him that she loved him. That she was sorry she'd ever chosen duty over love. Sorry she'd ever doubted his courage and honor. She wanted to tell him that she was sorry she'd never given them the chance to raise their children…

But it was too late. Too late for anything. Her body took over. She opened her mouth and took a deep breath of the water.

It seized her lungs, drowning her.

Her body collapsed in a seizure and the world went black.

Paolo felt her die in his arms as he wrenched her free.

Carrying her through the water, he used every

bit of his strength to reach the shore. But as he put her down on the slim margin of white sandy beach beyond the tide he knew it was too late. He'd lost her.

No.

He dropped to his knees. Turning her on her side, he pounded on her back. He rolled her faceup against the sand. He gave her two quick breaths, then started chest compressions, counting aloud. More breaths. More compressions.

She didn't respond.

She was gone.

"No!" he screamed.

He pounded her back, cursing at her, shouting at her. Finally he just crushed her against his chest as a sob rose in his throat he couldn't control.

"Don't," he whispered. "Don't leave me…"

He looked down at her pale, beautiful, lifeless face.

Suddenly she drew in a shuddering breath.

She coughed, then fell back onto the sand, retching seawater.

She looked up at him wanly, pale as a ghost. "Paolo…"

Tears streamed unchecked down his face as he stared at a living, breathing miracle. "Isabelle. You came back."

"I'm pregnant," she choked out. "You deserve to know. And no matter how long it takes for you to forgive me—"

"I forgive you." He silenced her with a gentle kiss. "I love you, Isabelle. I was a fool. All I can hope now is that you'll forgive me for failing to protect you…"

"You didn't fail!" she said indignantly. "I'm alive!" Weak as a kitten, she coughed more saltwater onto the sand, then shook her head, sagging against his soaking wet chest. "At least I *think* I'm alive. I must be. Everything hurts."

He looked into her beautiful face, so bright

with life, and at that instant it was like a lifetime of missed Christmas mornings distilled into one perfect moment of joy. "I'll call the doctor to make sure."

She snorted out a weak laugh, then clutched his shirt. "I'm sorry, Paolo. Sorry I ever doubted you. I will never doubt you again. I love you…"

"How touching."

Durand's sneer caused them both to look up. He stood high above them, pointing his pistol at them from the edge of the cliff. "Since you love her so much, Caretti, I'll let you decide. Which one of you should I shoot first? You, or the Princess?"

Cold fury ripped through Paolo.

"Let her go, Durand." He rose slowly to his feet, stepping in front of Isabelle, who was still too weak to rise. "You have your money," he said fiercely. "Let her go."

"So all the *carabiniers* can hunt me down like a criminal for the rest of my life? I don't think so." He raised the pistol. "Which one first? You have thirty seconds to decide."

Paolo took a deep breath, clenching his fists. He knew he could rush the cliffs and take his chance with Durand at close range, but that would leave Isabelle and his unborn child vulnerable and unprotected on the sand.

That left only one choice…

He spoke in a low voice, for Isabelle's ears alone. "When he shoots me, try and make it to the water. Swim out to where he can't reach you."

"No," she gasped. "No…"

"Save our child." He looked down at her and smiled. "Tell him about me."

"No!" she whimpered.

"Time's up," Durand said.

"Shoot me," Paolo said.

"No!" Isabelle screamed.

But as Durand aimed his pistol Paolo saw a sudden flash of movement and color behind him. Two hulking shadows rushed him, and Durand was suddenly the one screaming.

"Over the side," a woman's cold voice commanded.

The rocks slid beneath Durand's feet. He tripped on the gorse, stumbling as the ground fell away beneath him. For a moment his hands lashed out, desperately trying to grab something other than air. The pistol fired into the sky, echoing against his long, loud scream as he fell.

The faithless bodyguard bounced against the rocks once, twice. His screaming stopped long before he was finally swallowed by the unforgiving sea.

Paolo recognized Isabelle's two bodyguards. An elegant gray-haired woman stood behind them, glaring at the sea with narrowed eyes, dignified and fierce with a mother's vengeful fury.

"No one hurts my daughter," the woman said. She looked at Paolo, then slowly smiled. "No one."

* * *

Two months later, Isabelle was pacing Alexander's private room inside the palace.

"Stop that, will you?" her husband said, glancing at her above his copy of the *Wall Street Journal*. "You're wearing tracks into the marble."

"I can't help it." Flopping into a chair—she'd grown happily accustomed to stretchy, comfortable clothes, and the large velvet maternity dress she'd worn to Alexander's coronation was no exception—she glared at him. "We're newlyweds. I'm pregnant. I'd think you'd be more sympathetic."

"We all deal with stress in different ways," he said mildly, flipping the page. "Right now I'm coping by reading the business page."

She nearly believed him—until she saw the way his sleek leather shoes were tapping the floor. He was as nervous as she.

When Alexander finally entered the room, they both leapt to their feet like recalcitrant schoolchildren facing the headmaster. Their son was no longer wearing the ancient jeweled crown that had so recently been placed on his head by the archbishop—that had already been reverently taken to the vault that held all the de Luceran crown jewels. But after seeing his solemn dignity that morning, when he'd been crowned in the cathedral in a coronation ceremony attended by royalty and heads of state from all over the world, Isabelle thought that even without the crown Alexander looked taller. Older. Somehow he'd gained the stature of inches and years within space of a single hour.

"I'm sorry I had to keep you both waiting," he said with a formal nod. "Please sit down."

"That's quite all right," Isabelle said, feeling awkward.

"We know you're busy," Paolo said, tapping his heel.

Once they were seated, Alexander sat back against his chair and folded his legs against the cushion. "I'm exhausted. I believe I'll send for some ice cream, if you don't mind."

"Of course," Paolo said.

Suddenly, Isabelle couldn't take it anymore. "Alexander, we have something we want to tell you." Licking her lips, she glanced over at Paolo.

He cleared his throat. "Yes. We do."

He looked back at her.

A lot of help he was, she thought in affectionate exasperation.

"What is it?" Alexander said. "Some problem with the factory?"

"No, the factory is fine," Paolo hastened to assure him. "We've hired half of San Piedro to get it done, and there's more new business every day."

"Then let me guess." The boy turned to her. "*Grandmère* has convinced you to have another wedding so she can turn it into a state occasion? I'll admit, Aunt Isabelle, that I was surprised you insisted on such a small ceremony. I was sure you'd be clamoring for the hugest wedding cake ever seen on earth."

Paolo snickered under his breath, no doubt remembering the four slices of chocolate cake she'd eaten last night in her first real pregnancy craving. But it was *his* fault she'd eaten so much, she thought indignantly. Paolo and her mother were in cahoots, always bringing her tempting treats to get her to eat a little more for the sake of the baby. It was a wonder that Isabelle still fit into anything at *all*.

Shaking her head with a sigh, she said, "Alexander, we've agonized about whether to tell you this, but—" she glanced at her husband "—we've decided the truth is always best. And so we have to tell you… That is, you should know…"

She looked helplessly at Paolo.

He reached over to take her hand. Immediately she relaxed. Ever since that day on the beach when he'd saved her life there had been no secrets between them. He was her protector, her lover, her husband. The father of her children. He comforted her in every way.

Except, of course, when he thrilled her. As he'd done in bed last night. Three times. She didn't know if it was pregnancy hormones, or the fact that he knew just how to touch her, but she couldn't get enough.

And, luckily for her, Paolo loved nothing more than bringing her to indecent shuddering satisfaction again and again…

She felt her cheeks go hot. He gave her a wicked answering grin that told her she'd have more to enjoy tonight than just dessert.

Then Paolo's face sobered. For a long moment they looked at each other, gathering strength.

He turned to face Alexander.

"The truth is, Alexander, you're our son," he said gently.

The boy stared at them, wide-eyed.

"I know this might be a bit of a shock," Paolo

said, then rubbed the back of his head. "I only found out about this a few months ago myself…"

Isabelle knelt before their child, touching his arm. "I know there's so much to explain, but please, you have to know that Maxim and Karin loved you. Just as we do."

"I know." He looked at them, blinking in surprise. "I just thought we weren't supposed to talk about it."

Isabelle fell back against her haunches. "You *know*? What do you mean, you know?"

"Mama and Papa told me the truth a few months before they died. They said I was old enough to know that you gave birth to me. But they said never to speak of it, that even though they loved me with all their hearts it had broken yours to give me up." He glanced at Paolo. "From the moment you saved me in that Provençal farmhouse I wondered if you might be my father. We look so much alike. I wanted to ask, but I'd given my parents my word. But now—" he gave a sudden, impish grin "—you're the ones who brought it up, so I'm free to discuss it as much as I like. But first—ice cream. All this business of ruling a nation is exhausting."

Isabelle watched her son as he rang the bell. When a servant came, he requested, "Ice cream for three. No." He glanced at Isabelle's curving belly. "Four."

Isabelle sat against her husband, watching their son in wonder. Alexander already knew. He'd known all along.

And she realized then that everything was going to be all right. Better than all right.

Paolo's arms wrapped around her, and she felt him kiss her cheek. "We're a family," he whispered. "That means forever."

"Forever," she agreed with a sigh.

And, leaning back against the man she

adored, she could hardly imagine anything better than living in a palace with the sexiest man on earth, the son they loved, and a baby on the way—all that, with cake and ice cream too.

Mills & Boon® Online

Discover more romance at
www.millsandboon.co.uk

 FREE online reads

 Books up to one
month before shops

 Browse our books
before you buy

...and much more!

For exclusive competitions and instant updates:

Like us on **facebook.com/romancehq**

Follow us on **twitter.com/millsandboonuk**

Join us on **community.millsandboon.co.uk**

Visit us Online — Sign up for our FREE eNewsletter at
www.millsandboon.co.uk

WEB/M&B/RTL4/LP